# THE UNEXPECTED LETTER

# Elizabeth Gail

## THE 10 UNEXPECTED LETTER

# HILDA STAHL

TYNDALE KiDS — Tyndale House Publishers, Inc.
Wheaton, Illinois

Visit Tyndale's exciting Web site at www.tyndale.com

Formerly titled *Elizabeth Gail and the Terrifying News*

Designed by Beth Sparkman

ISBN 0-8423-4073-4, paper

Printed in the United States of America

08  07  06  05  04  03  02
10  9  8  7  6  5  4  3  2  1

*Dedicated with love to
Bob, Iva, John, Adam,
and Samantha Tol*

# CONTENTS

❀ ❀ ❀

# A Letter from Grandma LaDere

LIBBY reached into the silver mailbox and pulled out the stack of mail. Rex, the big black-and-tan collie, pressed tightly against Libby's bare legs. She shook her head at him as she closed the mailbox lid. "It's too hot, Rex. Why don't you lie down in the shade?"

He panted and wagged his tail as he stayed beside Libby all the way up the long driveway to the big house.

Libby frowned as she looked around the yard. Goosy Poosy usually ran to anyone who walked outdoors. Where was he? Then she saw the family's pet goose under a lilac bush, trying to hide from the heat. Libby was glad she could walk into the air-conditioned house to cool off instead of lying under a lilac bush. She patted Rex and once again told him to lie down in the shade; then she walked into the cool back porch. Thankfully, the family room felt even cooler.

"Any mail, Elizabeth?" asked Vera, looking up from a book she was reading as she sat curled up on the end of the couch.

"A big pile, Mom." Libby handed the mail to Vera, then stopped, her hazel eyes wide. "You called me Elizabeth!"

Vera chuckled. "That's your name, isn't it?"

Libby looked down at her bare toes and felt all long arms and legs. Yes, Elizabeth Gail Dobbs was her name, but Vera had called her Libby from the first day that Miss Miller had brought Libby to the Johnson farm to live.

Vera caught Libby's hand and squeezed it. "I didn't mean to embarrass you, Elizabeth. I just decided that since Chuck and the boys call you Elizabeth, I will too. It's a beautiful name."

Libby was glad that Vera hadn't added "for a beautiful girl" because she knew she was tall and skinny and ugly. Libby looked at Vera and smiled. "I like to be called Elizabeth."

"I'll try my best to remember. Libby is a

nice nickname and I like it, but since you like *Elizabeth* more, I'll call you Elizabeth." Vera looked down at the pile of mail and Libby sat cross-legged on the floor in front of her.

Maybe she'd have a letter from Mark McCall again today. Libby locked her fingers together and leaned forward expectantly.

"Here's a letter for you, Libby." Vera grinned sheepishly. "Elizabeth. I've never seen this handwriting before."

Libby's heart beat faster, and suddenly her hands felt too sticky to touch the white envelope. Maybe the letter was from her real mother. No! Oh no! It couldn't be from Mother!

Slowly Libby opened the letter and lifted out the single page with just a few words written in a strange, uneven handwriting. She looked at the signature at the bottom of the letter. Her hazel eyes widened and her heart leaped. "Mom! It's from Grandma LaDere! My very, very first letter from my real grandma!"

Vera's hand fluttered at her throat. "What does she say? I'm sure you're glad that she finally answered your many letters."

Libby read the few words. She cried out in

terror, her heart racing until she could not breathe, her hands stiff and frozen on the letter.

Vera slipped to the floor beside Libby and cradled her close. "Don't be frightened, honey. You are right here with me and nothing can hurt you." Gently she eased the letter from Libby's fingers and read it aloud: "'Elizabeth Gail, Marie got home two days ago. She is coming to get you. I wanted to warn you.'" It was signed "Ruth LaDere."

Libby watched the color drain from Vera's face. Vera was frightened too! Vera must think Mother would be able to come here and take her! With a moan Libby flung her arms around Vera and buried her face in Vera's neck. Mother would not get her away from the Johnson family! She was part of them now, after all these months.

"Calm down, Elizabeth," said Vera softly as she held Libby tightly. "I was startled and frightened for a minute, but not anymore. Now listen to me. Your mother cannot take you away from us. The court put you in our charge. Are you listening to me, Elizabeth? You are safe."

Libby pulled free and leaped to her feet, her chest heaving. "I am not safe with Mother so close again! She will take me again. I know she will!" Libby stared around the room as if her mother would walk in any minute and steal her away. Libby jumped in fright as Susan walked in from the kitchen.

"What's wrong?" asked Susan, staring from Vera to Libby with a puzzled frown. "Are you in more trouble, Libby?"

"Susan!" Vera frowned at her and shook her head.

"My mother is coming to take me!" cried Libby, pressing her hands to her heart. "Grandma LaDere said so!"

Susan's blue eyes widened in alarm, and she clapped her hands to her gaping mouth. Her red-gold hair hung long down her slender shoulders and back.

"Susan! Elizabeth!" Vera grasped each girl by an arm and led them to the couch. "We're going to sit down and talk about this. You're both too frightened to think." She waited until all three of them were seated on the couch. "Marie Dobbs cannot take you, Elizabeth, unless the court awards her custody of you. I don't believe they'll do that because of how she treated you in the past. Remember just after you came to live with us, Marie Dobbs wanted you to spend Christmas with

5

her. She didn't even stay for an answer. She went to Australia without another word. Maybe she told her mother that she was going to visit you without having any intentions of doing it."

"That's right, Libby," said Susan, nodding until her hair swirled around her head. "Your real mother won't come here. She hasn't so far. Why would she now?"

Libby shrugged, suddenly feeling cold. Her teeth chattered and she huddled closer to Vera. Dare she believe what Vera and Susan were saying?

Thunder crackled loudly and Libby jumped.

Ben burst into the room. "Mom! I just heard a severe-weather warning on the radio."

Vera jumped up and nervously pushed her blonde hair back from her face. "See to the animals, Ben. Susan and Libby, you'll have to help."

Libby pushed herself off the couch; her legs felt like rubber. How could she go outdoors and work? Maybe Mother was hiding in the barn or behind the chicken coop!

"Libby!" Vera shook Libby gently. "You must help. You don't want the animals to suffer, do you?"

Libby could not force herself to move. She

heard Ben ask what was wrong with her. Susan's voice seemed to come from a long way off as she answered Ben.

"You will not faint, Elizabeth!" Vera's face seemed to float in front of Libby. "Have you forgotten that you have a heavenly Father who cares for you? He loves you, Elizabeth! He will protect you!"

The words seemed to sink deep inside her, and Libby lifted her head as strength began to flow through her. In the past she had had to fight Mother by herself. Now she had the Johnson family and she had her heavenly Father.

"Susan and I will take care of everything by ourselves," said Ben.

Libby could see his concern for her in his eyes. She reached out and took his hand, then smiled weakly. He stood just a little taller than she did. His hair was very red and hers ordinary brown. "I can help, Ben," Libby said.

Thunder cracked again.

Ben grinned and squeezed Libby's hand. "We'd better hurry. We don't want to get caught in the rain."

Libby rushed outdoors into the wind. Already the temperature had dropped. Light-

7

ning zigzagged across the sky and thunder continued to roll.

"I'll take care of the chickens and Goosy Poosy," shouted Susan as she ran toward the chicken pen.

Anxiously Libby looked around the yard. Was her mother hiding behind one of the large trees in the front yard?

"Get Snowball, Elizabeth," called Ben against the wind.

Snowball! She was afraid of storms. Libby raced to the horse pen for her white filly. She could not leave Snowball outside in this storm.

Wind whipped Libby's short hair back and pushed her blue blouse against her thin body. She dare not think about Mother right now. The animals had to be put into the barns.

Frantically Libby worked with Ben and Susan till all the chores were done and all the animals were safe. The rain fell just as they ran back into the house.

Ben fought to hold the door open until Libby and Susan ran inside. The wind blew even harder and bent the trees until they were almost doubled over. Rain lashed against the windows.

Libby pressed her hands tightly against her heart. The storm outside echoed perfectly how she felt inside. Mother was home! Mother wanted to take her back!

Elizabeth Phil
Mama got home to
am. She is r...

# Rachael
# Avery

LIBBY clung tightly to Chuck as she sobbed out her terrible news as soon as he got home from work. She wanted him to take her far away where her mother would never find them. But maybe he would let Mother take her. Libby shuddered and clung even tighter.

Carefully he eased her back and looked into her tearstained face. "I will not allow your mother to take you from us, Elizabeth." He sounded so firm, so sure, that Libby once again felt a flicker of hope.

He gently wiped away her tears. She noticed that rain clung to his red hair and the shoulders of his jacket.

"Elizabeth, you belong to us. We want you with us. The court will not allow your mother

to take you. You are here to stay, Elizabeth."
When he smiled, tiny laugh lines spread from
the corners of his eyes to his hairline. "We
prayed you into our home, and we will not let
you go!" He shrugged out of his jacket and
hung it up. "We will not worry about your
mother. She can't harm any of us."

Libby hugged Chuck's arm as they walked
into the family room. With Chuck beside her,
she didn't feel quite so afraid.

Vera walked in from the kitchen, drying her
hands. She kissed Chuck, then talked to him
about Libby's problem. He reassured her, and
Libby could tell that Chuck made Vera feel
better too.

With a relieved smile Vera turned to Libby.
"I heard some good news today, Elizabeth. I
received a letter from Rachael Avery that
should make you very excited." Vera picked
up a letter from the end of the table next to
the couch. "I would have told you sooner, but
I didn't think you could listen with your
grandma's letter on your mind."

"What is it, Mom? Who's Rachael Avery?"
Libby could tell that Vera was suppressing
excitement.

"Is this news we should sit down for?"
asked Chuck with a grin.

Vera wrinkled her nose at him, then turned back to Libby. "Rachael Avery is the concert pianist I told you about a few weeks ago. She is taking students now that she's staying home to take care of her baby. I wrote and asked for an appointment for you."

Libby's fingers ached from gripping them together so tightly. Her heart seemed to have stopped beating and she could barely breathe. Could such a wonderful thing really be happening to her?

Vera rested her hands on Libby's narrow shoulders. "This does not mean that she'll take you as a student. This only means you can play for her, and then she'll decide if she is willing to teach you."

Libby looked deep into Vera's eyes. Did Vera think she had the talent? Could her dream of becoming a concert pianist really come true?

"When is the appointment?" asked Chuck excitedly. "I want to be in on this!"

Vera hesitated and Libby felt very nervous. What was Vera thinking about? Libby closed her eyes and tried to calm her thinking.

"After the letter from Ruth LaDere today

13

I didn't want to make the appointment until I talked to you, Chuck."

"Call her right now and make it as soon as possible."

Libby wanted to leap around the room and shout loudly, but she stood very still and waited. Could this really be happening to *her*, to a welfare kid? Next to being adopted by the Johnson family, her greatest dream was to be a concert pianist and play for thousands of people.

How hard it was to stand still and listen to Vera's end of the conversation when she called Rachael Avery. When Vera hung up the phone and turned to her, Libby felt light-headed.

Vera's blue eyes sparkled, and she looked almost as young as Susan. "It's tomorrow at four."

Libby stared at Vera, then down at her fingers. She could not play tomorrow! It was too soon! Libby flexed her fingers. They were stiff and wouldn't do what she wanted them to do. How could she play in front of Rachael Avery tomorrow?

Chuck gently took Libby's hands in his and spread her fingers on his. "You can do it, Elizabeth. You have a natural talent for the piano.

14

And you work hard. Think about your dream. Many people have dreams, but when it's time to turn the dream into reality, they panic. You will not allow fear to keep you from going after your dream. You can do it, Elizabeth. You'll see. You won't be alone. Mom and I will be with you. Jesus will be, too."

Libby lifted her pointed chin and squared her shoulders. "I will play for Rachael Avery tomorrow, and I'll play my best!"


Just before four the next afternoon, Libby walked with Vera and Chuck from their car to the front door of the house where Rachael Avery lived. Libby liked the house. It wasn't small and it wasn't as big as the Johnsons' house. A sprinkler watered the grass in the front yard, making it look a rich, deep green. Flowers bloomed on either side of the front walk.

Libby licked her dry lips and clutched her piano book tighter as Chuck pressed the doorbell. The chiming melody floated out to them. Were Chuck and Vera even a little nervous? Libby felt nervous enough for all three of them.

A tall, black-haired woman with smiling green eyes opened the door. She smiled warmly. "I'm Rachael Avery. And you must be Elizabeth Johnson."

Libby looked quickly at Chuck, then smiled at the woman.

"I hope you don't mind that we both came with Elizabeth," said Chuck with a smile. "This is a big occasion in our girl's life. We wanted to share it with her."

"Just have a seat. I'll take Elizabeth into the music room; then we'll talk later." Rachael Avery smiled at Libby and showed her where to go. She asked to be called Rachael because it made everything more friendly and relaxed.

Libby stared wide-eyed at the baby grand piano, then around the beautiful room, which was decorated with musical instruments, framed sheets of music, and pictures of Rachael in concert. Plants hung near each window.

"Sit down, Elizabeth." Rachael waited until Libby sat down on the piano bench. Then she sat on a stool next to the piano. "Now, tell me about yourself."

Libby locked her hands in her lap and wished she were back on the farm right now with Susan and Ben and Toby and Kevin. What could she tell Rachael?

16

"Don't be nervous, Elizabeth. I want to know about your dreams and ambitions. Just how much do you like the piano?"

Libby relaxed. Her eyes sparkled as she softly touched the keys. "I love the piano! Someday I want to play for thousands of people. I want to share the music that I feel inside with them." She turned to Rachael. Libby's cheeks were flushed a bright pink and her hazel eyes glowed.

"The piano talks to me," Libby continued. "When I feel sad, the music cheers me up. I can think right when I sit down and play. But I can't always get my fingers to move where my heart tells them to. I'm 12 years old. I haven't been taking lessons very long. Oh, but I want to play! I want to play!" Suddenly Libby stopped. Why had she told her innermost feelings to this stranger? How embarrassing! Quickly she looked down at her hands. A tight band seemed to be squeezing her chest. Why had she talked so much?

"Elizabeth." Rachael's voice was soft and warm. "I know the feeling. I always wanted to play just the way you mean. I played like that, and nothing came between my piano and me. Nothing until I met Martin. We have a six-month-old baby now. Martin and Seth are my life now instead of the piano. But I could not let my years of learning be lost. I can train others to do what I had dreamed of doing. Play for me, Elizabeth."

Libby took a deep breath. With trembling fingers she found the page that she had practiced for Rachael Avery. This could be the most important day in her life!

Libby touched the keys as she silently thanked Jesus that he was with her, helping her. She played, wishing she could play better, wishing she had started lessons when she was five or six.

At the end of the song she turned to Rachael and waited anxiously. She had fumbled once. But would Rachael know she was a little nervous and not count the mistake?

Rachael pushed her dark hair back with a long, slender hand. "You do have a long way to go to be a concert pianist, Elizabeth. But you have talent and you have a dream."

Libby locked her fingers tightly.

"I will talk to your parents before I decide."

Libby licked her dry lips. Did that mean she had a chance? Or was that Rachael's way of turning her down easily?

Rachael stood and placed her hand lightly

on Libby's shoulder. "You stay here and play just for your own pleasure while I talk to your parents. I'll call you in a few minutes."

Libby could only nod. How she wanted to follow Rachael and listen! She wiped her damp palms down her dress and then turned to another page of music. She would play so she would forget the waiting and the anxious moments.

Someday she would have a music room like this with a baby grand piano in it. She would practice all day long without having anyone stop her to do chores or go to school.

Libby thought of the tiny baby grand that sat on her dresser at home in her bedroom. Her friend Joe Wilkens had given it to her when Toby Smart had had a special party on the day of his adoption. Joe had said that Toby was getting gifts and he wanted Libby to have something too.

Libby smiled dreamily. Joe was nice. She liked him. He would be glad for her if Rachael asked her to be a student. Libby finished the song and sat back. It would be wonderful to have Rachael as a teacher.

Libby jumped in surprise as Rachael walked into the room. Libby studied Rachael's face for a sign of her answer. "Let's

talk together with your parents, Elizabeth."
She sounded very serious and Libby felt
frightened as she walked into the front room
beside Rachael.

Chuck reached for Libby's hand and pulled
her down beside him on the cream-colored
sofa. She leaned against him, waiting . . . waiting.

Rachael sat on a chair across from Chuck,
Vera, and Libby. "I asked about your back-
ground, Elizabeth."

The words made Libby freeze inside. Now
that Rachael knew she was nothing more than
a welfare kid she wouldn't take her as a
student.

"I understand that you have outside pressures that could keep your mind off your
piano."

Libby knew she meant Mother. Oh, why
hadn't Mother stayed in Australia?

"But, Elizabeth, I feel that your dream is
bigger than the pressures." Rachael paused, a
smile lighting up her attractive face. "I will
take you as a student."

Libby's eyes widened and she could not
believe her ears. She wanted to leap but
Chuck had a firm grip on her hand.

"But . . . ," continued Rachael, and Libby's

heart pounded in her chest. "I will stop the lessons if I see that you do not practice as you should. If anything comes between you and your piano, you will no longer be my pupil."

With a deep sigh Libby stood to her feet. She knew Mother would try to stop her. But she wasn't going to let that happen!

# Surprise Homecoming

LIBBY stood up and pressed her hands firmly against the small of her back. She hated picking string beans. She wanted to be in the house practicing the music that Rachael had assigned at her first piano lesson yesterday.

"Hurry up, Libby," said Susan sharply from the row of beans next to Libby. "We don't want to be out here all day long, you know."

"I *am* hurrying!" Libby wanted to walk out of the garden and stay out. Ben loved working in the garden. Kevin and Toby liked selling the produce at their roadside stand. Oh, why had she agreed to help? After this, her fingers would be too stiff to play the piano.

Reluctantly Libby bent down over the beans. She had promised to help. She would

not break her promise. Ben helped with the
birthday parties that she and Susan gave. She
could help Ben with his garden. But it was
very hard work!

Finally Libby lifted her basket of green
beans and carried it out of the garden into the
yard, where Ben divided them into quart and
half-bushel baskets. Maybe now she could
practice her piano.

She looked up as a big silver car stopped
beside the garage. Libby frowned, then
laughed in delight.

Grandma Feuder and Adam were climbing
out of the car, along with a man and woman
that Libby didn't know.

"Grandma! Adam!" Libby laughed excitedly as she ran to them. Grandma Feuder
lived just down the road from them. She
wasn't really their grandma, but everyone
called her Grandma. Adam was her great-
grandson.

Grandma's blue eyes sparkled and the
wind tugged at her white hair as she hugged
Libby close. She smelled like peppermint
candy.

Libby turned to Adam. She wanted to hug
him too, but she suddenly felt shy. She had
changed so much since she'd seen him last.

He smiled at her and asked how she was. She wanted to sink through the ground. She was glad Susan and Ben joined them so Adam wouldn't look at her anymore.

Grandma Feuder rested her hands on the man and woman on either side of her. "Children, this is my grandson Jim and his wife, Shirley. They're Adam's parents."

Libby liked Jim's smile as Grandma told a little about them. But when Libby looked at Shirley, the smile froze on her lips. She was surprised at the hate she saw in Shirley's eyes. Why would Adam's mother dislike her? Was she dirty after working in the garden? Or maybe Shirley didn't want a foster kid to be friends with her son. Libby stepped closer to Susan.

"We'll go in and talk to Vera," said Grandma Feuder. "Adam, you stay to help the children."

"Okay." He grinned. Libby had never seen him look so happy. His brown eyes glowed. His skin was almost as dark as Mark McCall's, and the sun had bleached his hair almost blond. As he talked about his stay with Bob Dupont, Libby studied him closely. She could look at him all day long and not be done looking. He had lost some of his thinness. Libby could see muscles developing in his arms and chest. Oh, it was good to see him again!

"I learned to drive a tractor while I was gone." Adam sounded very proud of himself, not at all like the selfish city boy he had been when Libby had first met him at Grandma Feuder's.

He asked about their summer, and Susan told him about giving birthday parties to make money. She told him about the fun times and left out the trouble they'd had with Gary Rousch. Adam listened as if he really wanted to hear. This Adam was not the same boy!

Libby smiled at Ben, and she knew he was thinking the same thing. He was remembering how he'd helped Adam accept Jesus as his Savior.

Just then Kevin raced down the driveway, his blond hair ruffled by the wind. He greeted Adam, then turned to Ben. "We're out of sweet corn and string beans. I have a customer who wants two dozen ears of corn." He took a deep breath and pushed his glasses against his round face.

"Here, Kevin." Ben picked up a basket of corn and handed it to Kevin. "We'll pick more in case anyone else needs it. Hurry back. Toby shouldn't be left alone."

Susan grabbed one side of the basket from Kevin. "I'll help you." She ran with him down the long driveway to the stand Chuck had helped the boys build.

"How's Snowball?" asked Adam, looking at Libby.

"She's growing fast, and she minds well now." Libby hesitated. Would Adam like to see Snowball? Or had he asked just to have something to say?

"Bob had a filly that looked almost like Snowball." Adam looked toward the horse pen. "I missed Snowball."

"Take Adam to see Snowball," said Ben as he bent to pick up the basket of string beans. "Adam, I'll see you later when I get done working."

Self-consciously, Libby ran with Adam to the fence. She called Snowball and watched proudly as the white filly ran to her.

"She *has* grown!" Adam stroked Snowball's face and talked to her quietly. Suddenly he turned to Libby. "How do you like my parents?"

Libby gripped the fence and kept her eyes glued to Snowball. "I just met them, Adam. How do you like having them back?"

He stood close beside her and she felt him

27

tense. "I don't know, Elizabeth. They're planning to stay with Grandma and me—until they want to go running off again." His voice sounded bitter.

Libby turned to him and wanted to take his hand in hers. "At least you know Grandma wants you, Adam. You will always have a home with her."

"Look at Ben and Susan. They never have to worry about a home or love or anything. They have it all!"

Libby pressed her hands together. "But look at me, Adam. And now my real mother wants to take me back!" Oh, she had not intended to say that! She had been forcing her thoughts away from Mother.

"What?" Adam's eyes widened and he looked sorry for Libby. "She can't do that, can she?"

"No! No, she can't! Dad says she can't! But, Adam, I get so scared! I want to stay here. I couldn't live without my new family and friends." She felt tears prick her eyes and she turned away quickly before Adam could see. She touched Snowball. "I couldn't live without Snowball."

"I'm sorry about your mother, Elizabeth. I wish I could help."

She forced a smile. "I have good news, Adam. I'm taking piano lessons from Rachael Avery in the city and she thinks I have promise."

"Rachael Avery! My mom knows her. We heard her in concert about two years ago. That's great, Elizabeth! You'll really learn to play well."

Just then Adam's family walked up to them. Excitedly, Adam told them about Libby's taking lessons from Rachael Avery. Libby could see the surprised look on Shirley Feuder's pale face. Jim Feuder clamped his hand on Libby's shoulder and told her he was happy for her. Libby managed a smile.

"I'd like to go back to the house and rest now," said Shirley tiredly. "Grandma, if you want to stay longer, then Jim can take me home and pick you up later."

Grandma patted Shirley's arm. "You go to the car and I'll be right there. I want just a word with Elizabeth." She slipped her arm around Libby's waist and waited until Shirley and Jim were walking toward the car.

Libby looked at Grandma, then blinked in surprise. She was as tall as Grandma Feuder! She had grown taller! She had been too busy to notice. Libby smiled into Grandma's eyes. Oh, it was good to have her home!

"How's Teddy, Elizabeth?"

Libby smiled happily. "Teddy is sitting on my bed right next to Pinky. I hug them both every night before I go to bed."

Adam groaned and rolled his eyes. "You sound as if a stuffed bear and dog are real. They aren't real animals, Elizabeth."

Libby gasped and pretended to be very hurt. "Why did you tell me that, Adam? I've been talking to them as old friends. And you tell me they're only stuffed animals! Oh, Adam!"

Adam and Grandma laughed.

"Teddy was my friend for years, Elizabeth," said Grandma with a twinkle in her eye. "I say he *is* a friend. I say he *is* real."

"Thank you." Libby turned to Adam. "I guess you were wrong, Adam. You don't know what you're talking about."

Adam laughed along with Libby and Grandma. Snowball nickered. Goosy Poosy honked indignantly from the chicken pen, where Kevin had locked him to keep him away from the customers.

"Adam! Grandma!" Shirley called impatiently from inside the big silver car. "Please, hurry! I must get home to rest."

Libby watched the laughter leave Adam's face, and she wanted to say something to bring it back.

"Coming, Shirley," called Grandma pleasantly. She turned to Libby. "Come see us as soon as you can. I've missed you." She hugged Libby quickly, then walked to the car with Adam.

At the car Adam looked back at Libby, waved, and climbed into the backseat. Everyone waved good-bye to Libby except Shirley. Libby leaned weakly against the fence. Why didn't Shirley Feuder like her?

"It's because I'm an ugly welfare kid," she muttered. Suddenly she gasped and her eyes widened. What if Shirley Feuder said something to Rachael Avery to make her change her mind about piano lessons? "She wouldn't! Oh, she wouldn't!" Libby muttered to herself.

Woodenly Libby walked to the house. Rachael would not dismiss her just because Shirley Feuder talked to her! Rachael *wanted* to give her lessons. "I have a dream," whispered Libby hoarsely. "I have a dream and I will do all I can to make it come true."

# The New Caseworker

"ELIZABETH!" Vera sounded very stern and Libby jumped.

Had Shirley Feuder said something to Vera? Libby swallowed hard. "What, Mom?"

"I just saw your room. Did you forget to clean it this morning?" Vera frowned as she stood at the foot of the stairs, her hands on her hips. "I have never seen it such a mess."

Libby flushed and stared down at her bare feet. "I . . . I forgot." She had meant to clean it the minute she'd practiced an hour on the piano. But then she'd helped Ben in the garden. "I'll go clean it now." How she wanted to sit at the piano and play until she forgot Shirley Feuder's dislike of her, forgot that Shirley might turn Rachael against her.

"Be sure to use window cleaner on your mirror." Vera moved away from the steps for Libby to pass. "Always clean your room before you come down each morning. That way it will stay clean."

The front doorbell rang, and Libby dashed upstairs as Vera answered.

Inside her room Libby looked around impatiently. Why hadn't she put her dirty clothes in the wash last night? She frowned at the lopsided way her pink bedspread hung off her bed.

She picked up Pinky and hugged him close, then smiled as she thought about Adam teasing her about Pinky and Teddy.

She lifted Pinky high. "I can't hug you all day, you know. I have to clean my room and practice my piano. Would you like to hear me play the piano? I'm much better than when I first started learning from Mom." Libby dropped Pinky on the big round hassock, then flipped her sheets and bedspread neatly into place.

Just as she finished dusting her desk and rubbing the wooden puzzle box from her father until it shone, Mom called upstairs to her. Libby frowned. Vera had ordered her to clean her room. Why would she call her now?

With a sigh and a shrug, Libby hurried into the hall, calling that she was coming. One of Vera's rules was to hurry to her when she called.

Libby stopped in the hall at the bottom of the steps. "I wasn't done yet . . ." Her voice trailed away at the strained look on Vera's face. "What is it?" Libby's words were barely audible over the sound of the grandfather clock's ticking.

"Your new caseworker is here." Vera touched Libby's arm; her hand was cold enough to make Libby shudder. "She's in the study. She wants to be called Ms. Kremeen."

Libby clung to the newel post. She could tell that Vera was upset with Ms. Kremeen. Oh, why hadn't Miss Miller stayed on as her caseworker? Uncle Luke shouldn't have married her and taken her away!

"She wants to talk to you alone, Elizabeth. I'll be in the family room if you need me." Vera squeezed Libby's arm, then released it. "Go on, Libby. Don't keep Ms. Kremeen waiting."

Libby wanted to turn and run back upstairs and hug Pinky and stay in her room until Ms. Kremeen left. She wished Chuck were home.

He would walk into the study with her even if Ms. Kremeen didn't want him there.

Slowly, reluctantly, Libby walked to the study. She stood at the closed door and remembered the times she had talked to Miss Miller in this very study. Now she had to meet a new caseworker. Would Ms. Kremeen like her? Libby suddenly pressed her hand over her mouth. Had her mother sent Ms. Kremeen?

Finally Libby pushed open the heavy oak door and walked into the study. She wanted to shrink out of sight as the tall, auburn-haired woman looked her up and down. Did she have pink lint all over her from her bedroom carpet?

Ms. Kremeen stepped forward. "I'm Ms. Kremeen. I've taken over your case from Gwen Miller Johnson. Have a chair, Libby." Her long hair swirled around her head as she walked behind the desk and sat on Chuck's chair. She folded her hands on the top of the large oak desk and studied Libby. Libby wanted to run from the room, but she sat perfectly still with her hands in her lap. Her long legs stuck out from her brown shorts and felt even longer than usual.

Libby could tell that Ms. Kremeen had long legs too, but hers were mostly covered by her soft yellow dress. What would Ms.

Kremeen say if she knew Libby was thinking about her long legs? Libby squirmed at the cold look in Ms. Kremeen's gray eyes. How Libby wanted Miss Miller back!

"Mrs. Johnson tells me that you are settled in. She is very happy with your progress." Ms. Kremeen studied Libby carefully. "Tell me how you like this home."

Libby lifted her chin and looked Ms. Kremeen right in the eye. "I love it here. This is my home. Someday the Johnsons will adopt me."

"Oh?"

Libby cringed at the sound and the look on the woman's face. "Just as soon as Mother signs the papers giving her permission, they'll adopt me."

"I don't believe you should say that as a definite statement of fact. Things are never that certain." Ms. Kremeen pushed her long hair back. "The Johnsons already have three children of their own and one adopted boy. The court may not approve another adoption."

Libby leaped to her feet, her hazel eyes flashing angrily. "Shut up! Shut up right now! I won't listen to you another minute!"

Ms. Kremeen stood up and walked angrily

around the desk, her fists knotted at her sides, her eyes blazing. "You will not talk to me in that manner, young lady. I shall look into having you placed in a home where you'll learn manners and not all this religious nonsense that Mrs. Johnson was talking about. Now sit down and stay there until this interview is over."

"You can't put me in another home! They prayed me here and I'm going to stay here!" Libby knew she should sit down and listen quietly to Ms. Kremeen, but she couldn't.

The door burst open and Vera rushed in. "What's wrong, Elizabeth?" She pulled Libby close. "What are you doing to this child, Ms. Kremeen?"

"Only telling her the truth, a thing you know nothing about, Mrs. Johnson. What have you told Libby about adopting her?"

"We mean to adopt her." Vera's voice was firm but Libby felt her shiver. "I will not allow you to say differently to her, Ms. Kremeen. You are only her caseworker, not the judge."

"What I say carries a lot of weight, Mrs. Johnson." Slowly she unclenched her fists and forced herself to lean back against the large desk. "I am sorry if I've offended in any way. That was not my intention."

Libby looked quickly at Vera. Did she know Ms. Kremeen was still angry even though it didn't show?

"If you have anything more to discuss with Elizabeth, then I shall insist on staying here with her." Vera kept a firm arm around Libby's waist while Libby leaned against her, glad for her support.

"I don't think I need to take any more of your time." Ms. Kremeen picked up a black briefcase and walked toward the door. "I will want to visit on a regular basis so I can satisfy myself that this is the best home for Libby."

"It is!" cried Libby. She wanted to say a whole lot more but Vera shushed her.

At the study door Ms. Kremeen turned and smiled coldly. "Marie Dobbs called me a few days ago."

The room seemed to spin. Libby had to lean hard against Vera to keep from falling.

"And did you tell Marie Dobbs that Elizabeth is staying right here with us?" asked Vera sharply.

"I told her I would investigate the case and report back to her." Ms. Kremeen smiled, a smile that did not reach her gray eyes. "I must warn you that my sympathy lies with the mother. Natural parents are always better for their children."

"Even when they mistreat them?" Vera sounded angry and Libby trembled. "Marie Dobbs was not good for Libby and never will be."

"Of course you are looking at this purely from your viewpoint, Mrs. Johnson."

Libby wanted to shout for Ms. Kremeen to shut up and leave, but she knew Vera would not approve.

Ms. Kremeen turned with a swish of her yellow dress. "I'll be back at unexpected moments."

Vera held Libby's hand as they walked Ms. Kremeen to the front door. Libby wanted to push the woman out and lock the door behind her.

Ms. Kremeen hesitated just outside the house. "Mrs. Johnson, I feel that for the good of the child you should discuss what will happen to her if you can never adopt her or if she goes to live with Marie Dobbs."

Vera lifted her chin and her eyes flashed. "I will do no such thing! We will adopt Elizabeth. I would like very much for you to take

Elizabeth off your work sheet and give her
case to someone else, perhaps Mrs. Blevins."

Libby frowned. Mrs. Blevins hated her
almost as much as Ms. Kremeen did.

"Mrs. Blevins would not take the case. I
have it and I mean to keep it."

Libby felt Vera shiver again. Where was
Goosy Poosy? Why didn't he come running
and knock Ms. Kremeen over?

Slowly Vera pushed the front door shut,
then leaned weakly against it. Tears slipped
down her pale cheeks. "I should not have lost
my temper with her. Now she will try harder
to get you away from us."

Libby's legs gave way, and she dropped to
the bottom step of the stairs. "Does this mean
I have to leave?"

"No! No, it does not!" Vera sat down beside
her, sniffing and wiping away her tears. "You
will not be taken away from us, Elizabeth!"

Just then Chuck walked in and stopped in
surprise when he saw them. "What's wrong
with you two?"

Libby leaped up and threw her arms around
him as she poured out the story. Vera inter-
rupted from time to time to add a thought.

"Hey, hey!" Chuck held Libby away from
him and looked from her to Vera. "Have you

both forgotten that we do not fight battles this way? We fight with prayer and God's Word. His Word says that nothing formed against us shall prosper. Ms. Kremeen cannot harm us. We prayed Elizabeth Gail into our house, and she will stay here!"

Libby stared into Chuck's face, clinging to every word he spoke. Could she believe him? Did he know how hard her mother and Ms. Kremeen would fight to get her away from this home?

"You sound so sure, Chuck," said Vera as she moved closer to him.

"I *am* sure." He smiled. "God is on our side. We are winners!"

Libby locked her fingers together tightly. She would believe what Chuck was saying. She would believe it with all her might! She had to or she would die.

# 5

# Birthday Party

LIBBY walked around the corner of the barn, then jumped back out of sight, her hazel eyes wide. Brenda Wilkens was standing in the yard talking to Susan. Today Libby could not stand Brenda's mean talk.

Rex pushed his nose against Libby's bare leg and she dropped beside him, hugging him close. "I'll stay right here until Brenda leaves," whispered Libby against the dog's neck. Maybe she should take Rex for a long, long walk so Brenda would be gone when she got back.

"Libby. Libby!"

It was Susan shouting for her. Libby wanted to cover her ears and pretend she

43

couldn't hear. Susan knew she didn't want to talk to or see Brenda Wilkens.

"Libby, come here quick!"

Libby's heart sank. Susan sounded desperate. What was Brenda doing to her?

Libby dashed around the barn toward Susan. Libby frowned. Susan didn't look hurt at all. And Brenda looked worried. For once she didn't stare right through Libby as if she weren't there or say something mean to her to hurt her.

Susan grabbed Libby's arm. "Brenda wants us to have a birthday party tomorrow for her cousin. Can we plan one for 10 people that fast?"

Libby thought about all the work they'd been doing and what little time she'd had to practice her piano. For two days after Ms. Kremeen had talked to her, she hadn't been able to practice. Her fingers had refused to play the right notes. Her mind had wandered from Ms. Kremeen to Mother.

"I'll help plan it and help with the work," said Brenda, locking and unlocking her fingers.

"Why can't we have the party Monday?" asked Libby.

"My cousin's birthday is tomorrow, and she

wants a party tomorrow." Brenda sounded as if she would burst into tears any minute. Libby had never seen her so upset.

"Brenda says her cousin is making a lot of trouble for her at home," said Susan. "She thinks this will help make things better."

Brenda pushed back her long dark hair with a quick nervous movement. "Mother is making me be nice to Allie." Tears filled Brenda's eyes. "Allie is mean to me and Mother doesn't know it. I told her and told her but she wouldn't believe me."

For one minute Libby felt glad that someone was mean to Brenda; then she was ashamed of herself. Jesus was teaching her to love Brenda. Love did not gloat over Brenda's unhappiness.

"Please, Libby, give a birthday party tomorrow for Allie." Tears slipped down Brenda's tanned cheek, and Libby knew she couldn't turn Brenda down.

"All right." Libby sighed because she really wanted to use the time to practice her piano. "We'll have the party tomorrow at two o'clock."

Susan laughed and hugged Libby. "We can't have it at two, Libby. We have to have it in the morning. Allie wants it that way."

"Thank you, Libby," said Brenda softly, and Libby almost fell over in surprise. Brenda had never spoken kindly to her.

Libby flushed and looked down at Rex. "Then we have a lot to do to be ready in time." A warm feeling spread inside her. She was doing something nice for Brenda. Finally Brenda was being kind. Maybe someday they would be friends. That was almost impossible to imagine!

"Are you going to stand here all day?" snapped Brenda, flipping her long dark hair over her slender shoulder. "We have work to do."

By 10 Saturday morning Libby felt as if she'd done three days' work. She leaned tiredly against the fence as Ben led Jack and Morgan into the driveway. The big gray draft horses looked extra handsome today with the polished brass-and-leather harness that hitched them to the big farm wagon. Maybe Allie hated horses.

Goosy Poosy honked from inside the chicken pen. Did he think he would have to spend the rest of his life in there?

"Have you met Allie yet, Ben?" asked Libby with a mischievous grin.

"No, but I saw her when I went over to talk to Joe last night." Ben chuckled as he pushed his hands deep into his jeans pockets. "She looks a lot like Brenda but she sure does act bossy."

"Even more than Brenda?" Libby laughed and held out her hand. "Don't get mad, Ben. I was only joking." She knew he liked Brenda. He didn't want anyone saying bad things about her.

"Joe says Allie thinks she's so much better than they are because she lives in the city and has everything she wants. Joe doesn't like her at all, but his mother makes him be nice to her." Ben's blue eyes twinkled. "Joe said he'd like to see you punch Allie in the nose like you did Brenda."

Libby flushed. She didn't want to remember that! She was trying her best not to punch anyone.

"Joe says she is always bragging about how many boyfriends she has. One of the reasons she wanted a birthday party so bad was to meet boys around here. She says if her parents mean for her to stay a month in the country, she wants to meet boys." Ben laughed. "I'm glad she thinks I'm too young for her. I wouldn't want her liking me."

"Besides, Brenda would be very jealous."
Libby thought of all the mean things Brenda
had said and done to her because of jealousy.
Could Allie really be worse than Brenda?

Ben nudged Libby. "Here they come. Oh,
look! Brenda was able to persuade Dave
Boomer to come. And he hates girls!" Ben
chuckled, then quickly covered it with a
cough.

Susan dashed out of the house just then,
and Libby and Susan greeted Allie with their
traditional birthday greeting. Libby could
see by Allie's face that she was very bored
and wanted to get on with it. She would
probably expect to play kissing games. Vera
had firmly said that it was forbidden.
Libby was glad. Who wanted to kiss a boy
anyway?

"Are we going on a hayride?" asked Allie
as she touched the side of the wagon. "That
should be fun. Come on, gang. Let's go
now!"

Libby frowned. She had wanted to play one
of the games first. She shrugged. Allie would
probably have considered the game childish,
anyway. "I'll go in the house and get Dad.
Everyone climb in and I'll be right back." She
was glad that Chuck had said he would drive

the wagon today. Allie could not pull any tricks with Chuck around.

Chuck looked up from watching cartoons with Kevin and Toby in the family room. "Ready to go already, Elizabeth? I wanted to watch the rest of this cartoon." Then he laughed. Libby knew he'd said that because the kids always said it to him.

"Just let me get my shoes and I'll be right with you."

Libby watched as Chuck stepped into his shoes, then tied them. He pushed his hair back off his forehead and said he was as ready as he'd ever be. "Do you think you'll get them to sing the songs you planned to sing?" asked Chuck as they walked out of the house and into the hot sun.

"Probably not." Libby grinned. "But we'll sure try."

Libby climbed into the wagon and sat beside Susan. Libby hid a grin as she saw that Allie was sitting between Dave and Tom. Larry and Ben sat on either side of Brenda. Penny had not come, so there were only nine people, ten with Chuck. Allie wouldn't miss Penny. She was too busy laughing and talking with Dave and Tom. Joe edged his way over and sat next to Libby.

"I think my cousin is having fun." Joe
grinned, and Libby thought he was better
looking than all the other boys.

"Is she going to church with you tomorrow?" asked Susan.

"Are you kidding?" Joe flushed, then
lowered his voice. "She thinks we are crazy
for going. It's just one more thing against us.
I sure wish she would've stayed home. We
don't need her."

"But maybe she needs you," said Susan
thoughtfully.

Libby studied Allie as Joe and Susan
talked. Did Allie have a hidden yearning for
God? Chuck often said that each person was
made to worship God. If they never found
him, then their lives were not complete. Did
Allie know that? Libby wanted to tell Allie
that God loved her. Oh, but wouldn't she
laugh? Silently Libby prayed for Allie.

"You're very quiet today, Elizabeth," said
Joe, looking at her with his warm brown eyes.
"Are you tired from working so hard on this
party?"

She shrugged. "A little. But I'm all right."
She smiled at Joe, then looked across and saw
Allie frowning at her. Was Allie mad because
she was talking to Joe?

"Let's sing," said Susan cheerfully. "We'll sing as we merrily roll along." She laughed, making her red-gold ponytail bob.

Libby joined in, but it was very hard to enjoy herself. She kept thinking about Allie not knowing God.

By the end of the birthday party Libby promised herself that she would find a chance to talk to Allie about Jesus. She had never talked to anyone like Allie about Jesus. She would pray. When she knew Jesus wanted her to talk to Allie, she would. Even if she was scared, she'd share Jesus with Allie.

# 6

# The Visitors

AS Libby loaded the dishwasher after lunch, she thought of what Connie Tol, her Sunday school teacher, had talked about last Sunday.

Connie had read about Jesus telling his disciples to go into the world and preach the gospel. Libby had not thought that meant she was to do it, but Connie had said that each person was to share Jesus with others. She had squirmed in her seat because she had not yet talked to Allie.

Libby closed the dishwasher and pressed the wash button. Water swooshed into the machine. She would ask the Lord to give her another chance to talk to Allie. She would ask Chuck what she should say, and she'd say it.

Dishes bumped and rattled as the dishwasher started up. A noisy car drove past outside. Piano music drifted into the kitchen from the family room where Vera was playing.

Libby leaned against the counter and listened to the music. She would learn to play as well as Vera. Libby frowned and looked down at her hands. She had practiced her lesson only 10 minutes yesterday. How could she go to her piano lesson Tuesday without practicing? Rachael Avery would be upset. And if Shirley Feuder had talked to her, then Rachael would have a good reason to stop giving Libby lessons.

Libby sighed and pressed her hands to her cheeks. Today and tomorrow she would practice. She would practice until her fingers dropped off!

The telephone rang and Libby jumped nervously. She picked it up and answered it.

"Elizabeth?"

Libby frowned. Was it Grandma Feuder? "Yes?"

"This is Ruth LaDere."

Libby sank into a kitchen chair, the phone gripped tightly in her hand and pressed hard against her ear. "Hello, Grandma LaDere." Libby thought her heart would jump right out of her chest. Her grandma had called her!

"How are you?" Libby wanted to ask what she wanted, but Vera had told her that it was not polite to ask that. "How's Albert?"

"Albert's fine. That crazy black dog chased him again. I had to get the fire department to get Albert out of the tree in the park. Albert scratched the man."

Libby listened as if she were in a dream. Maybe she *was* dreaming. Grandma LaDere would not call her.

"I didn't call to talk about Albert or me." Grandma's voice was sharp and impatient. "Marie left here this morning. She is going to get you back. I told her to leave you be, but she wouldn't listen to me."

Libby could barely breathe. The kitchen seemed to spin.

"Did you hear me, Elizabeth?"

Libby nodded. "Yes." Her voice was almost too weak to be heard. At the sound of the dial tone she realized that Grandma LaDere had hung up without saying good-bye.

In a daze Libby rose to her feet and hung up the phone. Was this a terrible nightmare? Would she wake up in her bed with Pinky snuggled in her arms?

Libby rubbed her hand on the smooth countertop. She touched a leaf of an ivy plant that hung in the window. Mother was coming to get her! Mother! "Dad!" Her voice rose as she called again and again.

"What's wrong, Elizabeth?" Chuck looked as if he'd just awakened from a nap.

Libby grabbed his shirt. "Dad. Oh, Dad!"

Chuck gathered her close and held her. "Calm down, Elizabeth. Tell me what has frightened you."

"Mother is coming here today!"

"How do you know?"

Haltingly Libby told him about the phone call. "I can't stay here another minute! I must hide!" She pressed her face against his shirt. She could smell his aftershave lotion.

He held her close as he talked to her, re-assuring her that Marie Dobbs could not just take her. "We won't allow her in this house. If she really does come, then I'll handle it. I won't even let her see you." He pushed Libby's hair from her face and wiped the tears from her eyes with his handkerchief. "Your mother talks a lot about coming here. But she hasn't yet. I don't think she will. Don't let her scare you like this."

The front doorbell rang and Libby gripped Chuck's arm. "She's here," whispered Libby hoarsely. "Mother is here!"

"We'll wait and see. Someone will answer the door, and if it is your mother, I'll take her outside and talk to her alone."

Libby listened intently as she pressed close to Chuck. Muted voices reached her ears, and she strained to catch the sound of her mother's voice. She could not hear it over the beating of Chuck's heart.

"Chuck, look who's here," called Vera from the hall. She sounded pleased. She would not be pleased if it was Mother.

Chuck sighed in relief and smiled at Libby. He lifted his eyebrows. "Shall we see who's here?"

Libby could only nod. On shaky legs she walked with Chuck to the family room. She blinked in surprise. It was Uncle Luke and Miss Miller—Libby stopped herself—Aunt Gwen, and Luke's son, Scottie, stood with Vera.

After noisy greetings, everyone settled in the family room to visit. Uncle Luke sat with Aunt Gwen on the sofa, his arm around her. Scottie sat on the floor with Kevin and Toby.

Uncle Luke talked about his job and how nice it was to have a wife to come home to each evening. Aunt Gwen blushed and said it was good to have a husband coming home to her.

Libby enjoyed listening, and she began to relax. She thought Aunt Gwen looked very pretty in her blue-flowered sundress and white sandals. She looked very happy. Was she glad that she didn't have to work in the Social Service Office anymore? Did she know Ms. Kremeen?

"We have a problem you might be able to help us with, Gwen." Chuck leaned forward, his face serious. "Marie Dobbs is trying to get Elizabeth back. I don't believe she can do it. I think Elizabeth would feel better hearing you say it."

Gwen shook her head as she looked sympathetically at Libby. "We have a complete history of your case at the office, Libby. No one would place you with your mother no matter how hard she tried to get you back."

"Mother is coming here today." Libby licked her dry lips and clenched her hands tightly together.

"She can't come here!" Gwen frowned. "She is not allowed to visit you except on very special occasions and then only with written permission. No, Libby, I don't believe she'd take a chance on coming to see you."

"Do you know Marla Kremeen?" asked Vera. "She's Libby's new caseworker."

Gwen frowned thoughtfully. "No, I don't believe I do."

Vera told how Ms. Kremeen had acted on her visit. Libby watched Gwen's face to see how she'd take that news.

"I think you should insist on a different caseworker, Vera."

Libby felt suddenly embarrassed. The conversation was too much on her. She felt like everyone was staring at her. She squirmed nervously and wanted to run to her room and hide. The longer they discussed her, the more agitated she became. She wanted to shout at them to stop talking about her and her case. She rubbed a damp palm down her jeans and tugged at the neck of her T-shirt.

"If you want, I'll go to the office tomorrow and talk to Mr. Cinder. He might have some answers." Gwen nodded thoughtfully, then glanced up at Luke. "We can stay in town long enough tomorrow, can't we?"

Luke nodded. "Sure we can. Anything to help our girl Libby."

Libby felt warm all over. It felt wonderful having Uncle Luke treat her as if she really was part of the family.

Finally, to her relief, Chuck changed the topic of conversation. Vera and Gwen excused themselves to fix coffee in the kitchen. Kevin, Toby, and Scottie ran noisily outdoors to play. Libby nervously twisted her fingers. Susan was reading her book again, and Ben was completely engrossed in his car manual.

Libby stared yearningly at the piano. She wanted to sit down on the piano bench and play until every thought was gone from her mind. She could push even her mother to the back of her mind if she could only play the piano.

The grandfather clock bonged four o'clock, and Libby jumped in surprise. It was almost time to start chores. Would Mother be waiting outside to snatch her? Why did Mother want her back now?

Gwen set a tray of sandwiches on the coffee table, telling everyone to help themselves.

Libby jumped up and walked with Gwen back to the kitchen. Libby smelled Gwen's perfume and remembered all the years she'd liked that smell. How mean she'd been to Miss Miller! Did Gwen remember and hate her?

Gwen slipped her arm around Libby's waist. "I'm sorry that you're having more trouble. I'll do everything I can to help you. You've found happiness and love after all these years, and I mean to see that you keep them!"

"Thank you." Tears stung Libby's eyes and she blinked them away. "I wanted Mother to stay in Australia forever!"

"I know, honey. But she's back and you have to deal with her. Learn from past troubles. It never pays to run away from problems. Face them and deal with them."

"I'll try, Aunt Gwen. But it's hard!"

"You have the entire Johnson family to stand with you. You have a loving heavenly Father who cares for you. Stand firm, Libby, and don't ever run, not even from your mother."

Slowly they walked back to the family room, each carrying a plate of chocolate chip cookies. They set them on the low coffee table.

The doorbell rang. The sound seemed to continue on and on inside Libby's head.

"I'll get it since I'm close," said Gwen.

Libby locked her icy fingers together behind her back. Her heart hammered so loudly that she was sure everyone could hear it. Could Mother be at the door?

Gwen pulled open the door. Heat from the outside rushed in. Libby saw a tall woman with bleached-blonde hair standing at the door. She was dressed in tight blue pants with a figure-hugging, yellow-and-blue tank top.

The blood drained from Libby's face and her knees turned to jelly. The woman at the door was Mother!

# 7

# Mother

"I WANT to see Libby." The woman stared, then stumbled back. "What are you doing here, Miss Miller?" Marie Dobbs's voice rasped against Libby's ears.

"What are *you* doing here, Mrs. Dobbs?" Gwen asked sharply. "You are violating the law."

"I'll handle this." Chuck squeezed Libby's shoulder reassuringly as he walked around her to the door. "I want to talk to you outside, Mrs. Dobbs."

Libby shivered and was glad when Vera pulled her close and held her tightly.

The door closed firmly behind Chuck and Mother as they headed outdoors. Libby's eyes blurred with tears as Aunt Gwen walked slowly toward her.

"I really didn't think she'd come here, Libby." Gwen looked as if she would burst into tears herself. Luke pulled her into his arms and held her.

"Let's go and sit down," said Luke firmly, leading Gwen to the sofa. He sat down and waited until Libby and Vera were seated also. "Chuck will take care of Marie Dobbs."

"What if she hurts him?" whispered Libby, gripping Vera's hand tightly. She remembered all the times Mother had beaten her. Was Chuck strong enough to stop Mother if she tried to beat him?

"Chuck can take care of himself, Elizabeth," said Luke. He rubbed his brown hair back and shook his head. "She sure does look like Phyllis LaDere. No wonder you were so scared when you saw Phyllis."

Libby thought about her visit to Grandma and Grandpa Johnson's when she'd first seen Phyllis and Tammy LaDere. It had been a very scary time. But having Mother right outside now was even worse.

"Luke, where is Scottie?" Gwen moved to the edge of the sofa. "I don't want him to hear the kind of language Marie Dobbs uses."

"I'll find him," said Ben, jumping up as he screwed the top on his container of paint.

"Have the boys come inside until Mrs. Dobbs leaves," said Vera. She sounded close to tears and Libby wanted to comfort her.

"I should have gone with Chuck to talk to her," said Gwen with a frown. "I could have helped."

"You'll be helping when you talk to Mr. Cinder tomorrow."

Just then the boys raced in, making too much noise for anyone to talk. Libby wanted to ask if they'd heard what was going on outdoors, but she didn't. She saw sympathy in Ben's eyes as he looked at her. What was he thinking? He might think Marie Dobbs would be able to take her away. Libby closed her eyes and leaned closer to Vera. Why didn't Chuck come back in?

About half an hour later Chuck walked in with a very satisfied smile on his face. He stood in the middle of the family room with his hands on his narrow hips and his red hair mussed from the hot wind.

"Marie Dobbs is gone! She says she missed Elizabeth so much that she just had to see her."

Libby chewed her lower lip nervously.

"But I read between the lines. Marie Dobbs is short on cash. And she knows if

65

Elizabeth lives with her she could get aid from Social Services. But I told her Elizabeth is here to stay."

Chuck flung back his head and laughed until everyone joined in. "I told her she might as well sign the adoption agreement now because we mean to adopt Elizabeth."

Libby pressed cold hands to her burning cheeks. With wide eyes she stared at Chuck.

"What did she say to that?" asked Vera eagerly.

"She said she'd think about it!" Chuck grabbed Libby's hands and pulled her to her feet. "Do you hear, Elizabeth? This is the closest we've come yet. She always flatly refused before." He looked around the room. "This is a time of rejoicing. I feel like thanking our heavenly Father for taking care of this."

Libby wanted to be as happy as everyone else as they thanked God for what he had done for them, but a tiny fear deep inside her kept her from feeling happy. Why couldn't she just push aside that fear and join in with the others? This was a time of celebration! She could be in Mother's car right now heading for town—away from the Johnsons and the farm. A smile tugged at her lips and finally broke through. She was still here! Mother was gone, at least for now. For that Libby was very thankful. Quietly she whispered thank you as Chuck continued to praise God.

"I feel like singing," said Susan gaily after Chuck's prayer. "Let's sing, shall we? I like to praise God by singing." With a happy smile Vera sat at the piano.

As they all gathered around the piano, Libby thought of the time she'd first come to live with the Johnsons. She'd made fun of the way they worshiped God, and now she joined in as if she'd always known the worship and praise songs.

Gwen caught Libby's eye and smiled. Libby knew Gwen was thinking how different Libby was now. Once she had called Miss Miller every dirty name she could think of. Now that same mouth was being used to worship God. Libby was glad she didn't say bad words anymore.

Did Mother ever think about God? Libby frowned and squirmed uncomfortably. She would not think about Mother right now!

Did Mother know that God loved her? Tears stung Libby's eyes. Frantically she pushed the thought away. No, she would not think about Mother!

Whoever prayed for Mother? Libby stopped singing and walked away from the group clustered around the piano. She stood beside the fireplace and stared at the empty grate. Why should she care who prayed for Mother? Mother was the enemy. She did not deserve to have anyone pray for her. She wanted to be the person she was.

But what if she didn't? Libby gasped at the thought. Her fingers trembled as she placed them on the top of the mantel. Grandma LaDere had never taught Mother to be different. Dad had walked out on Mother. He couldn't teach her about love or God or anything good.

Vera played one of Libby's favorite songs, but Libby could not sing around the hard lump in her throat. Could she really be feeling sorry for Mother? How could that be? Mother was mean and uncaring.

Had anyone ever really loved Mother?

Libby moved over to the coffee table and sank down on it. She would *not* think about Mother! But if no one ever loved Mother, how could she know how to love?

Libby looked up to find Chuck studying her. He smiled and lifted an eyebrow as if to ask her what was troubling her. She looked down quickly. What would he say if he knew what she'd been thinking? Would he be angry?

Chuck took her hand and lifted her up to stand beside him. When the song had ended, before anyone could suggest another one, he said, "I think this would be a very good time to pray for Marie Dobbs. God loves her just as much as he loves us. He wants her to know of his love."

Libby gasped in surprise. Had Chuck read her mind?

Chuck looked down at her. "Do you mind if we pray for her?"

She shook her head with tears in her eyes. How could this new family of hers be so full of love?

Chuck pulled her close to his side, then prayed for Marie Dobbs.

Tears slipped down Libby's cheeks and she let them fall. She heard Vera ask God to forgive her for hating and fearing Marie Dobbs. Libby blinked and rubbed her nose with the back of her hand. Should she ask God to forgive her for hating and fearing her mother? Oh, no! She could not do that! Mother deserved to be hated! She had to be feared! But then why had Vera asked God to forgive her for hating and fearing Mother? It was very strange. Libby shrugged. Vera could, but *she* never would!

Several minutes later Chuck sent Libby with the other children out to do the chores. Libby was glad Uncle Luke and Aunt Gwen were staying for supper.

Scottie slipped his hand into Libby's as they walked across the yard to the barn. "Why don't you have the same last name as we do, Libby?" Scottie looked up at Libby with wide blue eyes. His baby-fine hair was being ruffled by the wind.

Libby searched frantically for the right thing to say to Scottie. "I was born in a different family, Scottie. But someday I will have the same last name as yours."

"Was the other lady that was here your mother?"

"Yes."

"I saw her crying."

A hard knot tightened in Libby's stomach. She did not want to talk about Mother. "Hey, Scottie, want to see the kittens in the barn?"

"Sure." His eyes sparkled. He let go of Libby's hand and dashed toward the barn.

Slowly Libby followed him. She would not think about or talk about Mother!

# Libby and Brenda

LIBBY leaned forward, her elbows on the kitchen table. What was Gwen saying to Vera on the phone? Libby could not read the looks that crossed Vera's face, and Vera's end of the conversation didn't make any sense.

Finally Vera hung up and turned to Libby. Vera pushed her blonde hair back from her face. "Gwen talked to Mr. Cinder about Ms. Kremeen and your mother. He said that Ms. Kremeen is well qualified for her job and he respects her judgment."

Libby shivered and folded her arms tightly across her thin chest. What did Mr. Cinder mean?

Slowly Vera pulled out a chair and sat down. She absently brushed crumbs off the tablecloth. "Mr. Cinder will not do anything about Ms. Kremeen. He won't have your case given to anyone else. But your mother's visiting you here is another thing! He said he would take action and see that she doesn't come here again."

Libby let out a long breath. She was safe for a while.

"Dad and I are going to meet with Ms. Kremeen and see if she will take herself off your case." Vera chewed on her lower lip. "Ms. Kremeen will not hurt us! We won't let her!"

Vera took Libby's hand in hers. "You go out now and help Susan in the flower garden. Don't worry about Ms. Kremeen or your mother. We both need to trust God to take care of everything."

Libby managed a smile. She wanted to tell Vera how glad she was to have parents who were fighting for her, who loved her. All she could do was mumble a soft thank-you. Would she ever be able to say what she really felt inside?

Just as she walked outdoors, Adam Feuder rode up on his bike. He stood the bike in the grass and called hello to Libby.

"Why did you come over?" Libby clamped

her mouth shut. Why had she asked such a dumb question? Couldn't she just say hello and ask him how he was? Would she ever learn to talk to others the way Susan did?

"Grandma said I could visit for a while. She said you'd probably be working in the garden and I'm to help." Adam grinned and Libby flushed.

"Susan and I have to weed the flower garden. Ben is working in the vegetable garden." She wanted him to stay with her but she knew he'd go to Ben. Adam walked around the house to the front yard. "Hi, Susan. Want some help?"

Susan sat back on her heels and looked up with a cheery smile. "I sure do! Just don't pull out the flowers or Mom will get mad."

Libby dropped to her knees beside the pansies as Susan and Adam teased back and forth. Libby hoped Adam would think her flushed face was from the hot sun and not because he was close.

"My mother visited with Rachael Avery yesterday, Elizabeth," said Adam, looking up from the weed he'd just pulled.

Libby jerked, almost fell over, and caught herself. One hand pressed against a pansy and smashed it. She pulled her hand away, then knelt on the ground and stared wide-eyed at Adam. "What did they talk about?"

Adam frowned. "I don't know. Mother said she enjoyed being with Rachael again."

"Did she mention me?" Libby caught her breath.

"Why would they talk about you?" asked Adam. "Mother didn't tell me what they said."

"Why should she talk about you, Libby?" asked Susan in a puzzled voice.

"She doesn't like me. I know she doesn't think I should take piano lessons from Rachael." Libby twisted her fingers until they hurt.

"Why should Mother care?" Adam sounded impatient and just a little hurt. "I think your imagination is running wild."

Libby lifted her pointed chin and stared at Adam. "I saw the way she looked at me, Adam. She knows I'm an just a welfare kid."

"You don't know what you're talking about!" Adam jumped to his feet. "You don't like anyone's mother because of the way your mother treated you."

Libby leaped up, her fists doubled at her sides. "I like Susan's mother."

"Don't start fighting, Libby," said Susan impatiently. "We have to get this work done."

"I'm not fighting," Libby said sharply. "Adam is!"

"I am not! You don't know what fighting is!" He shook his head. "I'm going to help Ben. I'll be more welcome over there." He spun around and dashed to the vegetable garden.

Tears pricked Libby's eyes as she quickly dropped down to pull vigorously at the weeds. Let Adam go work with Ben. See if she cared! And if Susan said one word, she'd leave the flower garden and do something else.

As Libby worked, her anger slowly disappeared. She should not have gotten angry with Adam. What was wrong with her? Adam was her friend. He hadn't said anything to make her mad. "Susan, I have to go talk to Adam. I'll be back in a minute."

"Adam already left. I saw him ride away a little while ago."

Libby felt like crying.

"Uh-oh. Here comes Brenda." Susan jumped to her feet. "I just thought of something I have to do in the house."

Libby was too surprised to call to her.

"Libby. Libby, I have to talk to you." Brenda's face was red from hurrying.

Libby almost fell over in surprise. Brenda Wilkens had to talk to her!

Brenda dropped to the grass beside Libby. Nervously she pulled a blade of grass and stripped it with her thumbnail. "Allie is awful! She's getting me into bad trouble."

Libby almost told Brenda to take her trouble with Allie home again, that she didn't want to hear about it or help with it. But the anguished look on Brenda's face made Libby feel sorry for her. "What has Allie done this time?"

Brenda pushed her long dark hair back. Tears sparkled in her eyes. And Libby knew they were real tears, not the put-on tears that Brenda used to get sympathy.

"Mother left me home with Allie while she went to work today. I told her that we should go to town to stay with Mrs. Cheevy, but she said we'd be all right on our own." Brenda hugged her knees tightly. "Allie invited two boys over for this afternoon. Oh, Libby, she invited Steve Marsh and Bill Justen!"

Libby gasped. The boys were high school drug users! "Tell Allie that they can't come over."

"I tried! But she won't listen. She thinks they're cute. She doesn't care if they use drugs! I don't know what to do. Joe is gone for the day. We're home all alone. What am I going to do?" Brenda rocked back and forth in agony.

Brenda looked down, then right into Libby's eyes. "You know about kids like Steve and Bill. You know how to handle them. I don't! I don't know what to do about Allie."

"Is Allie using drugs?"

"No! At least she says she's not. She says she just wants to have some fun."

"She won't have fun with Steve Marsh and Bill Justen! They'll be trouble for sure!" Libby narrowed her eyes and stared across the yard. What could she do to help Brenda? Suddenly a smile tugged at her mouth. *She* was actually trying to help Brenda Wilkens! "Why don't you and Allie come over here? When the boys go to your house, nobody would be home."

"I couldn't get Allie over here," wailed Brenda. "She *wants* to have those boys come over."

"Let's go talk to Mom. She might know what to do." Libby jumped to her feet, but Brenda jerked her back down.

"You can't tell Mrs. Johnson. She might tell Mother. Allie said if my mother found out, she'd just say it was my idea. And Allie can lie until anyone believes her."

Libby remembered all the lies Brenda had told about her, and for just a minute she was glad that Brenda was having the same trouble. Libby pushed the feeling away. She would not be glad that Brenda was in trouble! Chuck had said that she should never feel that way.

"Does Allie know you're here?"

Brenda shook her head. "She was taking a long bath. I called down here but Mrs. Johnson said you were out working and that you'd call me back. I had to have help. What can I do?"

Libby grinned as an idea popped into her head. "You go home. What time are those boys supposed to be there?"

"About two."

"Okay. About two we'll come over to your house and visit you and Allie just long enough for those boys to get mad and leave."

Brenda's face brightened. "Allie will get so mad, but she can't blame me. Oh, Libby! Thank you!"

Libby flushed with pleasure. It felt wonderful to have Brenda thanking her. Maybe she and Brenda could be friends. She watched Brenda get on her bike and ride quickly away.

Suddenly Libby had a terrible thought.

What if Brenda was lying? Maybe she wanted Libby and the Johnson kids to get in trouble. Then Libby shook her head. Brenda had not been making up a story. She really did need help.

At 1:55 Libby looked around to see if everyone was ready. She smiled at Adam; she was glad that she'd called him and apologized for getting mad. When he smiled back at her, she felt warm all over.

Kevin and Toby could barely stand still as they asked Libby if it was time to go yet.

Ben grabbed Libby's arm. "There's Steve's car headed for the Wilkens place. We'll give them one minute and then go."

Susan giggled and bounced around excitedly. "This is better than TV."

"Time to go," said Libby breathlessly.

By the time they reached Brenda's house, Steve's car was empty and no one was in sight. Libby pressed the doorbell and waited. Wouldn't Allie be surprised to see a houseful of company instead of just two boys?

Finally Brenda opened the door and stepped back for them to enter. She looked very glad to see them.

Ben walked right into the front room where Allie and the boys were sitting. "Hi," he said with a wide grin. "I took time off from my roadside stand to come visit. How are you, Steve? Bill? Do you guys have summer jobs?"

Libby watched Allie's face turn red with anger. She tried to shut Ben up, and when she couldn't, she grabbed Brenda and led her aside. Libby couldn't hear what she said to Brenda, but she knew it was plenty.

Kevin and Toby asked Steve and Bill if they would go outdoors and pitch them a few balls.

"I'm going to public school this year," said Adam. "Bill, can you tell me about the school? Do they have a swim team?"

Libby hid a smile behind her hand at the exasperated looks on Steve's and Bill's faces. She knew that they would soon get tired of all of this and walk out.

Allie approached Steve and pulled him to his feet. "Let's go for a ride, shall we?"

"Great!" cried Kevin. "I wanted to ride in your car. Toby and me get the front seat!"

"No, Kevin," said Libby sternly. "Susan and I get the front seat. You have to sit in the back with the others."

Steve pulled free of Allie. "We've got to be going. Come on, Bill."

"Can you come again tomorrow?" asked

Allie, running after them. "We'll be alone tomorrow."

"Maybe tomorrow," said Steve, but Libby knew they'd never bother coming back.

Brenda turned and mouthed a thank-you to all of them.

Allie stormed back into the room, her dark eyes snapping. "I want all of you out right now! Do you hear?"

"Adam and Ben could stay," said Brenda.

"No!" Allie knotted her fists at her sides. "Nobody stays!"

Noisily Kevin and Toby ran out first and then the others followed. Toby walked beside Susan and could barely hold back a laugh.

# Piano
# Lesson

LIBBY waved good-bye to Vera, then slowly
walked to Rachael Avery's door. Nervously
she pushed the doorbell. Maybe Rachael
wouldn't be home. Maybe she would tell
Libby to come again another day when she
had more time.

Libby licked her dry lips and clutched her
piano books tighter. She had not practiced
enough. The week had sped by.

The door opened and Rachael greeted
Libby cheerfully. She was dressed in green
slacks and a lighter green blouse with tiny
white buttons down the front.

"Isn't this a beautiful day, Elizabeth? It's
not as hot as it has been." Rachael's voice was
pleasant to Libby's ears and she relaxed a
little.

Libby wanted to ask if Shirley Feuder had told her not to give her lessons, but she didn't dare. She sat on the piano bench, propped the music in place, and wished again that she'd practiced more. Nervously she rubbed her sweaty palms down her tan pants. She tugged her T-shirt down and wished she were at home going swimming with Ben and Susan.

"Relax, Elizabeth." Rachael patted Libby's shoulder. "Just play the songs I assigned you."

With a deep breath, Libby touched the keys, then fumbled through the first song.

"Try it again, Elizabeth. I don't understand why you are so nervous today. Do I scare you that much?"

Libby shook her head and tried again. Tears stung her eyes but she blinked them away. She would do the best she could.

"No. No, no, Elizabeth!" Rachael leaned forward in her chair with a frown on her attractive face. "You're doing that wrong. Look right here." She pointed to a note. "You are playing a *G.* That is an *A.* And the timing is wrong. It's like this." Rachael counted while she beat out the time with a pencil.

Libby wanted to hide under the piano.

"I'm sorry, Rachael," she whispered in embarrassment. "I . . . I didn't practice enough."

Rachael frowned. "I can see that. I warned you about outside things hindering you. If you can't practice, you are wasting my time and yours, as well as your parents' money."

"I know." Libby hunched her shoulders and dropped her head. "I did not have time. But I'll try this week."

"Elizabeth, you have a dream. To accomplish your desire you must work hard. Nothing can stand in your way."

"I know." Libby swallowed the hard lump in her throat.

Rachael rested her hand on Libby's shoulder. "Don't get so upset that you can't play today. I want you to know the importance of practice. If for some reason you feel that you can't practice, then tell me. We can stop lessons and resume them when you are up to it."

Libby lifted her head, her eyes wide in alarm. "I can't stop taking lessons! I will practice! I promise."

"You have set a long-term goal for yourself, Elizabeth, but each day you must set a smaller goal in order to reach the big goal. Be sure that you have an hour a day to practice, two if possible. Soon we'll make it four hours."

Libby groaned. How could she find four hours to practice?

"When other children are outdoors playing, you'll be inside practicing. Can you handle that?"

Libby winced. Could she? If Adam or Joe came by her house to go horseback riding, could she say no so she could practice?

"Not everyone has as big a dream as you have, Elizabeth. The bigger the dream, the harder you must work to attain it. You must ask yourself if you are really willing to work that hard."

Libby thought about it and finally she nodded yes. It was the hardest thing she'd ever had to agree to, but she knew she'd keep her word.

"And if you go back to live with your mother, what then?"

Libby gasped. "I'll never go live with Mother!"

Rachael lifted her eyebrows. "I understood that you might."

"I won't! Shirley Feuder hates me. She'd say anything to make trouble for me."

"That's a little harsh, isn't it? Shirley only mentioned that she knew you, so I asked her some questions. She told me what had been happening."

Libby looked Rachael right in the eye. "Will you make me stop taking lessons after what you learned about me? Do you think because I'm a welfare kid I can't learn piano?"

"Calm down, Elizabeth. I am not judging you by who you are or what you are. I chose you as a student because of your ability." Rachael gestured with her slim hands. "I want to keep you as a student as long as you practice the way you are told to. Even if you went back to your mother, I'd keep you on if she would bring you in."

"I am staying with the Johnsons!" Libby twisted around on the bench. "I have two dreams, Rachael. One is to be Elizabeth Gail Johnson. The other is to be a concert pianist. Both dreams will come true." Libby turned away, her face flushed red. Rachael Avery would not want to hear about her dreams to be adopted by the Johnsons.

"Elizabeth, you have a fighting spirit. And it takes one to reach your goals. Don't ever give up!"

Libby noticed the intensity of Rachael's

voice. Was Rachael sorry that she had a husband and baby?

"I want you to take the same music this week. I don't want to give it to you again, so please practice. Now, let's go over it. I want you to get it right this time."

Libby felt stiff and tired when the doorbell rang, telling her Vera had come to pick her up after her lesson.

"Shall I talk to Mrs. Johnson about seeing that you have more time to practice?" asked Rachael as they walked to the front door.

"No. I'll practice. I'll find the time. See you next Tuesday."

Rachael stopped Libby at the door. "You're a fine girl, Elizabeth. I want only the best for you."

Libby smiled self-consciously, then pulled the door open and walked out.

"How did the lesson go?" asked Vera as they walked to the car at the curb.

"Not too good, but it'll be better next week." Libby climbed into the car and looked up at Rachael's house. Rachael waved from her front window and Libby waved back. Rachael really was her friend. Shirley Feuder could not do anything to stop the lessons.

Even Mother couldn't stop them. Libby leaned back with a sigh.

Vera drove down the quiet street and pulled onto the main highway. "I saw Ms. Kremeen in the grocery store."

Libby turned to stare at Vera. "What did she say?"

"I made an appointment with her for tomorrow to talk about taking her off your case. She said she was willing to talk about it."

Libby let out a long sigh. "I'm so glad!"

"It doesn't mean that she'll agree with us, but at least we'll be able to discuss it." Vera stopped at a red light, then turned right.

"Aren't we going home?" Libby looked around in surprise. To go home Vera should have turned left.

"While we're in town I thought it would be fun to stop at the store to see Chuck. I told him we might."

Libby smiled. She liked visiting Chuck in his store. He would let her look at the merchandise and choose something that she wanted. Since it was a general store, there was a lot to choose from.

Chuck's clerk, Lucy Pennock, met them just inside the door. She greeted them with a cheery hello and a happy smile. "Chuck is in his office with a customer right now. I'm sure he'll be out soon."

Libby walked slowly down the aisles as Vera and Lucy talked. She found a pack of colored felt-tip markers that she liked. Maybe she'd take those if Chuck said she could choose something. She saw some pink nail polish that she knew Susan would like. She stopped to look at stuffed animals just outside Chuck's office. A woman's familiar voice inside made her turn around and stare in fright at the half-closed door.

Mother was talking to Chuck!

Libby looked around wildly. Where could she hide? Her legs felt too weak to carry her anywhere. A hand gripped her arm and she cried out in alarm, then relaxed when she saw it was Vera. "Mother is in the office," whispered Libby huskily. "What will we do?"

Vera's face turned almost as white as her sleeveless blouse. She led Libby away from the office. "We'll wait over there where she can't see us when she comes out."

"Anything wrong?" asked Lucy anxiously.

"We're going to sit down in the shoe department. When Chuck is free, we'll talk to him."

Libby barely made it to the chair before her legs gave way. She gripped the arms of the chair and took a steadying breath. Was Mother saying bad things to Chuck?

"Try to relax, Elizabeth," Vera said softly. "Dad can handle your mother. She's probably trying again to talk him into giving you up. But we'll never do that."

Libby closed her eyes tightly. How she hated Mother! She should have stayed in Australia!

Several minutes later Libby felt a light kiss on her forehead. She opened her eyes, then threw her arms around Chuck's neck. "What did Mother want this time?"

Chuck grinned. "Same as before. I told her to give up. She is very persistent and stubborn."

"Aren't you worried?" asked Libby breathlessly.

"Not a bit. I was glad for the chance to talk to her. I told her how you are growing in the Lord. She was at a loss for words for almost an entire minute."

Vera moved closer to Chuck and Libby. "Do you think she'll come back in here to bother you again?"

Chuck kissed the tip of Vera's nose. "She

might, but it won't bother me. I asked the Lord to give me a chance to tell her about God's love. I started today, but she walked off in a huff."

Libby squirmed uncomfortably. She did not want to talk about Mother. It was better just to pretend she didn't exist. "Can we go home, Mom?"

"Don't you want to stay with me?" asked Chuck, smiling at her.

"No. I don't want to see Mother. She might come in again."

"We'll see you later, Chuck. Why don't you ask Lucy to lock up for you so you can come home early."

"I will. See you later." He kissed Vera, then Libby.

Libby walked quickly to the car and slumped down on the front seat. She did not want to see Mother or have Mother see her.

# 10

# Ms. Kremeen

LIBBY stood up from the piano bench with a satisfied smile. "That was good, wasn't it, Mom?"

Vera nodded as she looked up from her embroidery. "The best you've done yet. Rachael will be very proud of you. If you practice as much every day as you did this afternoon, you'll have your lesson perfect."

"Now can I turn on the TV?" asked Susan from the chair where she'd been reading.

"For a while, Susan." Vera stood up and stretched. "I'll go start supper. Elizabeth, would you like to help?"

Libby nodded. She liked to cook.

The doorbell rang just as Libby stepped into the hall. She looked startled and scared.

Could it be Mother? After talking to Chuck in his store, had she driven out to see Libby?

"Don't panic, Elizabeth," said Vera softly as she walked around Libby to open the door. "Ms. Kremeen! What a surprise. Our appointment was for tomorrow, not this afternoon."

"May I come in?" She sounded so smug, so sure of herself, that Libby wanted to turn and run.

Vera stepped aside and Ms. Kremeen walked inside. She barely smiled at Libby.

"What can I do for you, Ms. Kremeen?" asked Vera coldly.

"Shall we talk in private?"

Libby could smell the social worker's perfume. It wasn't nice like Aunt Gwen's always was. Ms. Kremeen's auburn hair was long and curly, and the pink dress she wore showed her figure too much. Libby wanted to tell her to leave and never come back. How she wanted Miss Miller!

Sounds of laughter came from the TV as Libby watched Ms. Kremeen follow Vera to the study. What did she want to say in private? Tomorrow was the appointment to discuss giving up her case. Why was Ms. Kremeen here now?

Slowly Libby walked toward the study

door. She noticed it had not latched shut. Carefully, with icy fingers, she pushed it open just enough to hear the conversation.

"I talked with Marie Dobbs about an hour ago, Mrs. Johnson."

"And?"

Libby pressed her hands over her heart to quiet the beating.

"Marie Dobbs is very sorry for the way she treated Libby in the past. She is ready to devote her entire life to making Libby happy. I believe her. I know that a child is better off with his or her own parents. I have studied several cases, and I can see in each one that it was psychologically better to have the child with the birth parent or parents."

Libby wanted to rush into the room and yell for Ms. Kremeen to shut up! Why didn't Vera kick her out? Or was Ms. Kremeen convincing Vera that it would be better for Libby to go back to Mother?

"You love Libby, Mrs. Johnson. I can see that you do. Don't you want what is best for her?"

"Ms. Kremeen, let me ask you something. Why are you working so hard to get Elizabeth away from us?"

"I am not working any harder on this case

than on any others. I only want what is best for Libby."

Libby made a face and stuck out her tongue at the door.

"I never get personally involved with my cases like Miss Miller did. I don't approve of that. If you don't get emotionally involved, then you can judge with a clear head what is best. I can see this case clearly. Libby needs to be with her mother."

A cold shiver ran down Libby's spine.

"And be beaten and starved again?" Vera argued. "And let's not forget she was abandoned or the fact that Libby knows more about life than any 12-year-old should know."

"Don't get hysterical, Mrs. Johnson. We are two adults discussing a case."

"No, Ms. Kremeen. I am a mother who loves her child. I am going to keep Elizabeth if I must fight forever to do it."

Libby wanted to hug Vera.

"I'm afraid you won't have much choice. I have already set in motion the action to return Libby to Marie Dobbs. Nothing you can do will stop it. Marie Dobbs will have Libby back with her in a very short time. I will be proud to say that I helped bring it about."

With a moan of agony Libby turned and ran

out of the house. She slammed the front door behind her. Rex barked and ran to her side, but she screamed at him to get away from her. She was going to run and run, and Rex could not go with her.

Snowball whinnied from the pen. Oh, she would never see Snowball again! Maybe she could just hide and sneak back when Ms. Kremeen gave up trying to get her back to Mother.

At the end of the driveway she turned left so she wouldn't have to talk to Ben at his roadside stand. He called to her, but she kept running. Pain shot through her side, and she slowed when she drew near Grandma Feuder's place. Lapdog ran out to meet her, barking a glad welcome.

"Elizabeth!" called Adam as if he was very glad to see her.

Libby gasped for breath. That's it! She would ask Adam to hide her. He would help her. He was her friend.

"What's wrong, Elizabeth? You look scared to death."

"Adam. Oh, Adam!" She clutched his arm and tried to catch her breath. "I need you to hide me. Ms. Kremeen came to take me back to Mother!"

"Oh, no! How can she do such a terrible thing? Come on. Sit down on the porch until you calm down. I'll get you a glass of cold water."

"I don't want your parents to know I'm here."

"Only Grandma's home. Now, just sit on the porch swing. I'll be right out with a glass of water."

She caught his hand. "Don't tell Grandma I'm here. She'll think she has to send me home."

Adam hesitated, then reluctantly agreed.

Lapdog jumped up and laid his head on Libby's lap. She pushed against the porch floor with her sandaled foot and closed her eyes. A gentle breeze cooled her and dried the perspiration from her face.

"Here's the water." Adam pushed the glass into her hand. "After you drink that we'll walk in back where no one can see us, and you can tell me what happened."

"You won't make me go home, will you?"

"Not if you don't want to. Drink the water."

Gratefully Libby drained the glass. She handed the empty glass to Adam and wiped her mouth with the back of her hand. She pushed herself up off the swing. Lapdog jumped to the floor and wriggled around her feet.

Adam set the glass beside the swing, then took Libby's hand. "Come on. We'll talk."

Just as they stepped off the porch a big silver car drove in. Libby looked over her shoulder in fear. Shirley and Jim Feuder were in the car and they'd seen her! "Let's go, Adam!"

"They won't say anything, Elizabeth. They won't hurt you."

She pulled her hand free and dashed toward the barn. She could hide in the small barn where Brenda had hidden Snowball in the spring.

Adam ran along beside her, telling her that he was going to help her if she'd just give him a chance. Finally he caught her arm and pulled her to a stop. "Now, tell me what's happened! If you don't, I'll take you home right now!" His brown eyes looked almost black and a twig was caught in his hair.

And Libby told him. She fought against the tears that were trying to fall. She did not want Adam to see her cry.

"I don't know what good it will do for you to run away, but I'll hide you for a while."

"Thank you. I know I could sleep in that small barn in the back of Grandma's place. You can bring me food and water. I could stay hidden for a long time."

"But school starts in 10 days. You can't hide then."

Libby lifted her pointed chin. "If I have to, I will." She thought of the pretty new school clothes Vera had helped her buy. She looked down at her worn jeans and T-shirt. Could she live in those clothes for a long time?

Once when she was five, Mother had left her in their apartment for three days by herself. She had kept the same pants and sweatshirt on every day and every night. Would it be just as scary alone in the barn now that she was 12 as it had been in the apartment when she was five? Now she had Adam to bring her food. Then, she'd had to eat whatever Mother had left in the refrigerator.

Quickly Libby pushed that memory away. She had been so hungry when Miss Miller had found her!

"Maybe you can bring out a sleeping bag for me, Adam."

"I'll try." He didn't sound happy that she was going to spend the night in the old barn.

Libby stopped in the clearing and looked at the weathered barn. Grandma had said it was over 100 years old. How many runaways had slept in it?

Thankfully Libby sank to the ground and leaned against the rough siding of the barn. A bee buzzed around her head, then flew away. Lapdog plopped down beside her, his tongue hanging out.

Adam talked quietly until Libby relaxed. Then Adam left to get her a sleeping bag and food.

Just a little fear fluttered inside her now. She jumped up and walked inside the barn. She could stay in here for a year if she had to. Adam would take care of her.

Sun filtered through wide cracks, making it easy to see inside. She touched the stall where Snowball had been tied. A mouse scurried across the dirt floor, and Libby jumped back in alarm. She had not thought about mice. Would a mouse chew on her while she slept?

She made a face. She brushed a cobweb away, hating the feel of it clinging to her. Maybe this was not such a good spot to stay.

At the sound of footsteps she looked up expectantly. Adam was coming back! Oh, she would be glad to see him. It was terrible being alone, even for a short time. Could she really stay alone at night—all night—for as many nights as she needed to stay?

She jumped back as Chuck walked into the barn. "How did you find me?" she cried, her hazel eyes full of alarm.

"Shirley Feuder called and told us you were here."

"I knew she'd tell! I just knew it!"

"I'm glad she did, Elizabeth." Chuck looked very stern. "Do you know how scared we were when we realized you'd actually run away? How many times must I tell you not to run away? It doesn't solve anything!"

"I won't go back to Mother!" Libby looked wildly around for a way of escape.

"Listen to me, Elizabeth." Chuck caught her by the arms and held her firmly. "You will not go back with your mother."

"But Ms. Kremeen said—"

"I don't care what she said! You are staying with us. Running away only complicates the situation. Don't do it again. Understand?"

Libby didn't really understand. So she just stared hopefully at Chuck, willing him to have an answer for her.

Chuck tried to reassure her as they walked

to the pickup parked in Grandma Feuder's driveway.

Just as Libby opened the pickup door, Adam ran to her. She glared at him and he jerked back in surprise. Just wait till she talked to Adam by herself! He'd be sorry that his mother told on her!

# 11

# Family Meeting

LIBBY pressed her back against the sofa and pulled her knees up under her chin. She just knew everyone in the family was staring at her, thinking she'd been really dumb to run away. Out of the corner of her eye she saw Chuck cross his legs and lean back in his chair. Did he hate her for running away?

"We're having this meeting to stop Ms. Kremeen from further action," said Chuck.

Libby looked at him and actually caught a smile on his face and a twinkle in his hazel eyes. This was serious business! Why was he treating it so lightly?

"I know what we should do," said Toby, jumping to his feet. He rubbed his hands across his freckled face. "We should lock the doors and not answer when she comes back."

Libby smiled weakly. She liked his idea.

"We're going to fight this battle in a different manner," said Chuck cheerfully. "We've been learning to put God's Word into action. Now is our chance!"

"You mean take our Bible and beat her over the head with it?" asked Kevin with a very straight face.

Libby looked around her in astonishment as everyone laughed. How could they laugh? She was in terrible danger!

"Let's get serious," said Vera. She reached out and patted Libby's shoulder. "We are going to keep our girl right here where she belongs."

Chuck uncrossed his legs and leaned forward. "Our enemy is not Ms. Kremeen. And our enemy is not Marie Dobbs."

Libby frowned. Chuck was so wrong!

"Our enemy is Satan!" Chuck waited and then continued. "Satan tries to keep believers in constant fear and confusion. God's Word says, 'the Spirit who lives in you is greater than the spirit who lives in the world.' Because we have God in us, we have the power to defeat Satan. Now we need to draw on that power and act like winners. We have to think like winners and talk like winners because we are God's children."

"How do we do that?" asked Ben with a frown.

"God's Word says that he will take care of his children." Chuck's warm laughter filled the room, and Libby felt the knot in her stomach ease just a little. "We will trust God that he is in control of Elizabeth's case, and we'll thank him for giving Elizabeth to us. We will pray that he stops Ms. Kremeen's legal actions and Marie Dobbs's harassment."

Chuck looked around eagerly. "Listen, everyone! God is powerful and he is on our side! He loves us. If at any time a wrong thought comes into our head, we will push it away and say that God is with us. We are victorious. Elizabeth is ours in Jesus' name. We will not allow thoughts of defeat to stay with us. Defeat is from Satan! Victory is from God! Our weapon is not going to be a judge deciding who is better for Elizabeth. Our weapons are speaking God's words and drawing on God's power through our prayers. In him we are *more* than conquerors!"

Libby could only stare at Chuck. Was he serious! Wasn't he going to see the judge and explain what was happening? Wasn't he going to kick Ms. Kremeen off her case?

Fighting with fists was something Libby could understand. Even fighting in a courtroom she could understand. But fighting with words? Libby shook her head hopelessly. Fighting with words would not work!

"I think you should explain how this will work, Chuck," said Vera.

Chuck pressed his fingertips together and looked at the others over the top of them. Libby dropped her eyes before he could read her thoughts.

"The words we speak are important. If we speak words of doubt and fear, Satan can use those words to defeat us. When we speak words of belief and victory, God will honor those words and bring to pass whatever is best for us. God has given us a powerful weapon: prayers full of faith-filled words. When we pray, believing in God's power to help us, he will. He will help us keep Elizabeth."

Libby listened as Ben, then Susan, added their own feelings. Libby knew she would fight a whole lot better if the Johnson family would fight for her in a different way—a way she could understand and help with.

Libby was glad when everyone was talked

out. She wanted to get to her room and be alone and think of a plan herself. She could not sit back and let Ms. Kremeen and Mother take her without a fight—the kind of fight she knew about.

"Time for bed, kids," said Vera, standing up and stretching. "I think I'm going to take a shower and go right to bed too. This has been a very exhausting day."

Libby pushed herself to her feet and walked toward the door. Chuck caught her wrist and she looked up at him in surprise. "I want to talk to you in the study," he said quietly.

Her heart dropped to her feet. She was in real trouble now! Hesitantly she walked ahead of him to the study. She wanted to run to her room and hide under the covers. She did not want to hear his scolding.

Chuck slipped his arm around her waist and pulled her down beside him on the leather sofa. Tears pricked her eyes and she blinked hard.

"Elizabeth, have you been able to forgive your mother for what she has done to you?"

Libby's eyes widened. She had not expected that question. She twisted around until she could see Chuck's face. "I will never forgive her! I hate her!"

He held her hand gently. "We are trying to live by God's Word, aren't we?"

She nodded.

"According to God's Word, we are to forgive as our Father forgave us. If we can't forgive others, he can't forgive us." Chuck rubbed the back of Libby's hand. "Remember how hard it was for you to forgive your real dad for walking out on you?"

Libby nodded again. It had been very hard.

"But God helped you to forgive him and love him. All the bitterness and hatred left. God put love inside you, love and forgiveness. Bad feelings are harmful, Elizabeth. They stop good communication between you and God. Bad feelings hurt *you,* honey. Do you think your mother is hurt because you hate her?"

Libby frowned. "Mother doesn't care how I feel."

"You are only hurting yourself by being unforgiving toward your mother. I know that we've talked about this often. You need to pray about this one again, then act on it."

Libby thought of the terrible things her mother had done to her. She could not love or forgive Mother! She did not want to!

Chuck squeezed Libby's hand. "Elizabeth,

I will pray that God gives you the right spirit toward your mother. I will not force you to say you forgive her or love her. I know that you will be able to see clearly what we have talked about tonight. You no longer see things with this world's eyes. You see things with a spiritual eye. You will see how Jesus wants you to act and talk. You'll do what Jesus wants you to do."

Libby lowered her eyes and studied Chuck's fingers. This time Chuck was wrong. She would not understand what he was saying. She would not try to love or forgive Mother.

"The fight with your mother will be over just as soon as you allow God to take care of the situation," said Chuck softly. "God wants to fight this battle for you, but you are trying to do it with your own strength and your own weapons. You'll see that only God's weapons will cause us to win."

Chuck kissed the tip of Libby's nose. "Go to bed now, honey. Sleep tight."

Libby hugged him, wishing she could stay right here, close to him forever, where she would always feel safe.

"I love you, Elizabeth."

"I love you, Dad."

Chuck took her face in his large hands.

"God loves you even more than I do. You can trust him even more than you trust me. You can lean on him always. Someday you will have to stand alone with God without me to help you. Don't be afraid when that time comes, honey. As you grow in the Lord, you'll find it is easier and easier to depend on the Lord."

Libby could only stare at Chuck. She couldn't imagine not depending on him. Since he said that God could be trusted, it must be true. Until that time, she would lean on Chuck for everything.

Chuck jumped up and pulled Libby to her feet. "Up to bed with you. See you in the morning."

"Good night, Dad." Reluctantly Libby walked away. It would be terrible if she didn't have Chuck for a dad. What would she have done if Miss Miller had taken her to a different home? That was too awful to think about.

Slowly Libby climbed the stairs and walked to her bedroom. She picked up Pinky and hugged him close. "Pinky, I have the best family in the whole entire world."

Later Libby climbed in between the cool sheets. She yawned widely and stretched out thankfully. It felt good to be in bed. This day had seemed four days long!

What would she say to Adam tomorrow when she saw him? Did he know his mother was a tattletale? Libby frowned as she thought of just what she would say to Adam and to his mother if she had a chance. Adam would be sorry!

A cold band tightened around Libby's heart, and tears filled her eyes. Adam was her friend. How could she be mean to him? She was just as bad as Mother!

"I forgive Adam," she whispered. She asked Jesus to forgive her for thinking about getting back at Adam.

Could she forgive Shirley Feuder?

Libby blinked. How could she think about forgiving Shirley? But did she want that bad feeling to stay inside her and turn her good feelings into rotten ones?

"Jesus, help me to forgive Shirley Feuder. She sure made me mad by telling Dad where I was, but I guess I'm glad he found me. I really didn't want to sleep in that barn all by myself."

Libby stopped, then smiled. She was talking to Jesus just like Chuck did.

Could she forgive Mother?

Libby frowned. That was impossible!

With a tired sigh, Libby turned on her side and closed her eyes. The sound of a whip-poorwill's call drifted through the window. "Thank you, heavenly Father, for the whip-poorwill," she whispered sleepily.

# 12

# Running Again

LIBBY patted Snowball one last time, then let her run back into the pen. Snowball was learning very well. Sometimes it was hard to find time to train her, to work with her the way Chuck had told Libby to. It was hard to decide what was more fun—training Snowball or practicing the piano.

Flies buzzed around Libby's head and she swatted impatiently at them. The afternoon sun almost blinded her as she walked out of the shade of the barn. She felt hot and sticky and dirty in her faded jeans and old blue work shirt. She twisted her foot inside her boot. Chuck insisted that everyone working with the horses had to wear boots just in case the horse stepped on a foot.

"Libby!"

Libby turned at the frantic whisper. She frowned. Brenda was hiding behind a tree and motioning frantically for her to come.

"What's wrong, Brenda?" asked Libby sharply. Brenda's face was actually dirty. Her dark hair was in tangles around her shoulders. Dark circles around her eyes made her look as if she hadn't slept in days.

"It's Allie again!" Brenda sounded as if she'd burst into tears any minute.

"Let's go to my room and talk."

Brenda jerked back and looked wildly around. "No! I can't let anyone see me. I look terrible!" Nervously she tugged her bright red T-shirt over her denim shorts. "Mother said I had to stay in my room all day! I sneaked out and Joe almost caught me. I had to run and hide and I got bit by bugs and I'm dirty and I feel awful!" Tears rolled down Brenda's cheeks and Libby felt sorry for her.

"Let's sit down in the grass behind the lilac bush where no one can see us." Libby walked Brenda to the spot and settled her down. "Tell me what happened."

"Allie wanted to go to the drive-in last night. Mother said we couldn't because it was showing an R-rated movie." Brenda pressed her arms against her chest. "But when Allie wants

116

to do something, she does it! We went with two boys who I didn't even know. When we got back home, Mother was waiting. Allie told her a wild story about me calling the boys and making plans to sneak out with them."

Brenda rocked back and forth as she went on. "Mother wouldn't believe me when I said I didn't do it. She said she had learned not to trust anything I said. And of course Allie plays like she's very obedient and nice in front of Mother, so Mother falls for it. Oh, Libby, I don't know what to do! Allie is driving me crazy!"

Libby almost told her she was getting just what she deserved, then forced away that thought. She had forgiven Brenda. With God's love in her she was loving Brenda. "Why don't you talk to Chuck or Vera? They'll know how to help you. Mom could talk to your mother and tell her about Allie."

Brenda jumped up and looked down haughtily at Libby. "You won't help me because I've been mean to you. That's all right with me. I don't need you anyway, welfare kid. I don't know why I thought you could help."

"Wait, Brenda." Libby leaped up and caught Brenda's arm. "I want to help you. I just don't know how. But I could try to pray with you."

Brenda jerked her arm away. "If I wanted prayer, I'd have called my Sunday school teacher!" She flipped back her tangled hair and ran across the yard toward the road.

Libby stood helplessly, her hands at her sides, her mouth open to call after Brenda.

"I've been waiting for you, Libby."

Libby turned, then stumbled back with a gasp. "Mother!" she exclaimed. "Where did you come from?"

"I parked my car on the road and walked up. I've been waiting for quite a while to get you alone."

Libby's heart thudded painfully. Fear pricked her skin. She backed away until she bumped against a tree. She tried to scream, but only a strangled moan escaped her lips.

"I'm not going to hurt you, Libby." Mother stepped close and smiled. The smile did not reach her blue eyes. A twig had caught in her bleached-blonde hair. Her ragged jeans and dirty T-shirt looked ready for the dump. "I want to talk quietly and calmly to you."

Numbly, Libby shook her head and she sank down to sit at the base of the tree. Where was Ben or Susan? she wondered. Didn't anyone know Mother was here?

"I need you, Libby." Marie Dobbs squatted in front of Libby. "I promise not to treat you bad. I've got a guy who wants to marry me if you will live with us. Ms. Kremeen says I can get you back. But you could make it easy for me. Just tell this family you don't want to live with them anymore. Tell Ms. Kremeen that you want to live with me. You're 12, going on 13. You could live anywhere you want by just saying so."

"I won't live with you," whispered Libby through dry lips. "I won't ever live with you again!"

Abruptly Marie Dobbs rose to her feet. "We'll see about that!" She grabbed Libby's wrist and jerked her to her feet. "I'll make you pay for this! When I do get you back, you'll be one very sorry kid!"

Libby shook violently. The last time Mother had looked like this she had beaten her with an extension cord, then locked her in the small, dusty broom closet. A neighbor had found her hours later and had taken her to the emergency room, where she'd stayed until Miss Miller picked her up.

"If I could, I'd make you go with me right now." Mother smiled wickedly. "But I'll get you back. Ms. Kremeen is very determined to set things right. And she thinks 'right' is having you live with me. I told her I'd let her handle it. She might be out today to get you."

Desperately Libby looked around. Was Ms. Kremeen already parked in the driveway ready to grab her?

Goosy Poosy honked and Mother jumped in surprise. "I'm getting out of here now. I'll see you soon, Libby." She walked away, her back straight, her steps sure. Libby could tell that Mother was sure everything would work out just the way she wanted.

Libby clenched her fists and lifted her head. Her eyes flashed. Mother would not get her back no matter what Ms. Kremeen said!

As strength returned to her legs Libby decided just where she would run to this time. She would not take a chance on hiding in the old barn at Grandma Feuder's. This time she would run back into the woods and hide there. She would worry about food later. At night she'd sneak back to the farm and sleep in the barn next to Snowball. No one would ever think that she'd stay nearby.

Cautiously Libby walked around the house and across to the horse barn. If it had a hayloft like the barn on Old Zeb's ranch, she could hide in it. Once she thought she heard someone calling her. She stopped behind a tree and listened. Rex barked twice, then stopped. She was glad he was tied up or he'd have followed her. It would have been hard to stay out of sight with Rex beside her, even though it would have been nice to have him with her so she wouldn't be lonely. Libby shrugged. This she had to do alone.

Tears blurred her vision as she ran through the field where they had taken children for wagon rides. Libby stopped. Tomorrow she and Susan were to give a birthday party for Marjorie Jaydeen! What would Susan do when she found Libby gone? Libby sighed and shook her head. Susan would have to give the party herself. Ben would help.

With her head down, Libby trudged through the tall grass. Flies buzzed around her head. A deerfly caught in her hair and wildly she swatted it out. A ground sparrow sang its pretty little song, then flew away. A big blue racer parted the grass at Libby's feet. She jumped and screamed and watched in horror as it slithered away. Finally her heart settled back in place and she walked on.

In the shade of the pines she sank down and caught her breath. How quiet and lonely it seemed all around her already. The only sounds were the birds in the trees, little animals scurrying around, and her own breathing. She pulled her knees up under her chin and hugged her legs to her.

What would Rachael Avery do when she didn't show up for her piano lesson Tuesday? Libby moaned. She did not want to think about this! She knew Rachael would drop her. Another boy or girl would gladly fill the spot she left vacant.

Was it really worth running away? Chuck had told her that running away didn't help anything. But staying would be worse if Ms. Kremeen took her back to her mother.

An ant crawled on Libby's arm and she brushed it off.

A movement to her right caught her attention. Someone was there! Had Mother followed her?

Libby leaped to her feet and ran into the pines, ducking under the low branches. Why hadn't she kept running? Oh, she could not be caught now!

The sun almost blinded her as she raced out of the pines into the clearing. Wildly she looked for a spot to hide. Ben's Christmas trees were not far away. Could she run fast enough to hide behind them before Mother made it through the pines?

Libby stumbled and sprawled hard on the ground. Whimpering in fear, she pushed herself up and raced toward Ben's Christmas trees. She did not dare look back in case she stumbled and fell again.

"Libby! Libby!"

"She's going to catch me," whimpered Libby as she ran harder. Pain shot through her side. Scalding tears spilled down her hot cheeks. She stumbled, caught herself, and raced on. She would have to run and run until she couldn't run another step.

A tree root caught her foot, and she stumbled forward into tall brush. Blood oozed down her cheek from a deep scratch made by a branch. She had to get up! She could not just lie still and be caught.

Weakly she pushed herself away from the brush. She could not move any farther. Mother had her! Mother would not give up until she dragged her to her car and kept her always!

A strong hand grabbed Libby's bare arm. Libby screamed in fear. She was caught!

# 13

# A New Friend

"WHAT'S wrong with you, Libby?"

Libby looked up and sagged in relief. "Brenda! Brenda, why were you chasing me?"

"I saw your mother talking to you. Ben told me about your trouble. I thought I could help you."

Libby's eyes widened. Brenda Wilkens wanted to help her?

"I followed you to see what you were going to do. I didn't mean to scare you." Brenda sank exhaustedly to the ground. Bloody scratches covered her bare legs. She touched a large welt on her arm where a bee had stung her. "Are you running away?"

Libby flushed and lowered her eyes. She did not want to answer that. "Why didn't you go home? Your mother is going to be very angry."

Brenda shrugged. "She already is." Brenda shifted into a more comfortable position. "I did think of something you could do to help me."

"What?" She couldn't do anything to help anybody. Brenda must know that.

"You could talk to my mom and tell her the truth about me. She would believe you, Libby."

"Talk to your mother? But she hates me!"

Brenda flushed and looked quickly away. "But she would believe you."

"I can't talk to her. I can't go back yet."

"The Johnsons will protect you."

"I know they'll try."

"I didn't think you really believed all that talk about God loving you and taking care of you."

Libby stared at Brenda. "I do believe it. I don't know why you say I don't."

Brenda frowned. "If you really believed it, you wouldn't be running away. You would believe that God can take care of you. You would have stayed at home and let God work things out."

"But . . . but . . ." Libby searched frantically

for something to say to that. Wasn't Brenda right after all? If she really trusted God to take care of her, wouldn't she have stayed home? Wouldn't she have fought the way Chuck had said to fight?

"I didn't say that to make you feel bad, Libby."

"I do feel bad." Libby nodded. "You're right, Brenda. If I really believed it, I wouldn't have run away again." Slowly she pushed herself to her feet. Her legs wobbled and she couldn't move for a minute. "I'm going home right now."

Brenda jumped up. "Come to my house first and talk to Mother for me. I don't want to stay in my room forever. I planned on horseback riding with Ben today."

Libby sighed. "I'll think about it, Brenda." And she had other things to think about, too, things that she'd been pushing to the back of her mind so she wouldn't have to consider them.

"What's wrong, Libby? You look sort of strange."

Libby was quiet for a long moment. Should she tell Brenda? "I've been wrong, Brenda. I really thought I could be a Christian and hate my mother for what she did to me. But I can't! I need to forgive Mother and love her with God's love. For myself, I need that."

"That doesn't make sense to me, Libby."

Libby walked slowly along until they reached the pines. She stopped and turned to Brenda. "I want God to answer my prayers and meet my needs, but I keep sinning. Dad told me that no matter what someone does to me I must forgive and love. If I don't, then I'm blocking myself from God. I want to be like Jesus, Brenda. Jesus always forgives and loves. And I must too."

"I would never forgive Allie!"

"I said I would never forgive Mother. But I'm going to, Brenda. I forgive Mother. I forgive her!" Tears stung Libby's eyes as a clean feeling swept through her. "I love Mother with God's love." Could she really love Mother? "I love Mother with God's love," she repeated.

Brenda shook her head. "I don't understand you, Libby. You can't love your mother after what she's done to you."

Libby laughed. Something Chuck had said came back to her. "God's Word doesn't say to love people who are good to you. His Word says to love everyone as he loves."

"Are you going to live with your mother again?"

"Oh, no! I wouldn't do that! God gave me the Johnson family as my family. I will stay with them." With a toss of her head Libby walked through the pines. She had to get home and tell Vera what she'd learned.

"Why don't you come to my house and stay there until you know it's safe at your house?" Brenda sounded worried, and for just a minute Libby felt that worry.

Chuck had said to get rid of any bad thoughts. She would get rid of worry! She would not think about being in danger. "I'll be all right, Brenda. Honest, I will. I know God is taking care of everything. I need to trust him. He will stop Ms. Kremeen. He will stop Mother."

"But how do you know?"

"God loves me, and he wants to take care of me."

Brenda touched Libby's arm. Libby stopped and turned questioningly to her. "Libby, does God love me?"

"Sure he does!"

"How do you know?"

"God loves everyone, Brenda. The Bible says so. The Bible is God's words to us. If he

129

*says* he loves you and me, then he *does* love you and me."

A tear slipped down Brenda's cheek. "Are you sure?"

Libby nodded. "I'm sure."

"Ben and I have had a lot of talks about Jesus. Ben said that Jesus can take away my sin and make me into the person God planned on me being. Do you think so too?"

Libby looked at Brenda carefully. "I know that Jesus loves you. He loves me. And you know he is changing me!"

Brenda tipped her head and studied Libby. "I know you're different than when you first came to live with the Johnsons. I know you hated everybody. And now you say you even love your mother. I hope you aren't putting on."

"I'm not. I know I'm different. If I weren't, I wouldn't be talking to you right now. I love you, Brenda. And I want to help you."

Brenda gasped. "You've told me lots of times that you hated me. You have never said that you loved me. How can you, Libby?"

"God is loving you through me. I don't know how it works. I just know it does."

"Libby, I want to be a Christian. I made fun of Joe when he became one, but I really

was jealous. I made fun of you, too, Libby.
I'm ashamed. I want you to forgive me."

Libby smiled. "I already did. You see, I had
to forgive you because Jesus wanted me to."

"I want to pray right now, Libby. I don't
want to wait until Sunday in church to be-
come a Christian. I want to do it right now."

Libby held her hand out to Brenda. Libby's
heart leaped for joy as Brenda took her hand.
"We'll pray together."

"I'm not good at saying a prayer."

"That's all right, Brenda." Libby felt like
shouting with joy as Brenda talked to Jesus.
And Brenda was serious. She was not pretend-
ing just so Libby would help her.

Finally Brenda looked at Libby. "I am a
Christian now. Jesus is my Savior. I didn't
think I'd feel different, but I do! Libby, I'm
not scared anymore. Maybe I can even like
Allie!" Brenda threw back her head and
laughed with delight. Libby had never heard
her laugh that way before. But she knew how
Brenda felt. And it was something to be
happy about.

"Won't Ben be excited when you tell him?"
asked Libby with a wide smile.

"I can't wait to tell him!" Brenda dashed
away, her long hair flowing behind her.

Libby laughed and ran along with Brenda. She could hardly wait to get home. The black cloud that had dropped over her the day Grandma LaDere had called with the terrifying news was gone.

By the time they reached the farmyard, Libby was hot and thirsty. She stopped at the outside faucet and turned on the cold water, letting it run over her hands and arms. She splashed her face, then cupped her hands and drank until the dryness in her throat was gone. She stood back as Brenda did the same thing. Was this the same Brenda who always looked neat and tidy? Libby wondered, looking at Brenda's sweaty face and tangled hair.

Libby turned with a smile as Susan ran up to them.

"Where have you been, Libby? Mom sent me to find you so you'd practice your piano."

"Tell Mom that I'm going to Brenda's for a while. As soon as I get back I'll practice." Libby laughed at the surprise on Susan's face.

Brenda pressed her hands together and laughed. "Susan, Libby and I have talked and prayed. I'm a Christian. I really am!"

Susan's mouth fell open and she stared wordlessly at Brenda.

"It's true, Susan," said Libby. "And Brenda is my friend now. Right, Brenda?"

Brenda nodded. "Yes, Libby. We're friends."

Libby grinned self-consciously.

"I can't wait to see Ben's face when he hears this news," said Susan, grinning broadly. "Here he comes now. I'm so excited!"

"What are you so excited about now, Susan?" asked Ben, returning Susan's grin.

"Let me tell," said Brenda, sounding as excited as Susan.

Libby watched the joy leap into Ben's face as Brenda talked. Had Ben prayed more for Brenda than the others had?

As they were talking and laughing together, a small green car drove up the driveway. Libby held her breath as Mrs. Wilkens and Allie climbed out of the car.

"What happened to you, Brenda?" cried Mrs. Wilkens in concern, looking her daughter up and down. "You look terrible!"

"I'm all right, Mother. I'm sorry if I scared you."

Libby saw Allie stare in surprise. Allie looked cool and pretty and very clean in her red shorts and red-and-white tank top. Her long dark hair was brushed as neatly as Brenda usually kept hers.

"I was worried sick. Allie said you weren't in your room."

"I sneaked out to come see Libby," said Brenda, nervously locking her fingers together. "I wanted her help."

"Did you have to get so messed up getting it?" asked Allie, looking down her nose at Brenda.

"She was trying to help me," said Libby, lifting her pointed chin. "I was running away from home so my mother couldn't take me. Brenda followed me to help me."

Mrs. Wilkens looked at the girls with a puzzled frown. "I don't understand what's happening."

"Let's go home, Mother. I'll tell you every-thing after I've had a warm shower." Brenda caught her mother's hand and tugged her toward the car.

"Do you still want me to help you, Brenda?" asked Libby.

Brenda smiled. "Not now, Libby. I'll call you if I do. I have a *new Friend* who will really help me a lot."

Libby smiled as Brenda climbed into the car with Mrs. Wilkens and Allie.

"I'm glad you came home, Elizabeth," said Ben.

"I am too, Ben." Libby walked toward the house. "I will never run away again." And she meant it. She no longer feared Mother or Ms. Kremeen. She belonged to God. She was his child, too, and he was taking very good care of her!

# 14

# Grandma LaDere to the Rescue

"I'M very proud of you, Elizabeth." Chuck wrapped his long arms around Libby and pulled her close. "I'm sorry that your mother gave you such a bad scare."

"I know that Mother can't take me away from you, Dad. I really know it!"

"Good for you, honey."

"Libby! Dad!" Susan stopped breathlessly in the family room doorway. "Ms. Kremeen just drove in. And Marie Dobbs is with her!" Susan's blue eyes were wide with alarm. She clenched and unclenched her hands.

Chuck pulled Susan close to his side. "Don't worry, Susan. God is in control. Remember? You don't need to fear."

Libby swallowed hard as Chuck reassured Susan. Libby felt panic sweep over her; then she pushed the feeling away. God *was* in control! She did not need to fear. Nothing that Ms. Kremeen or Mother could do would harm her.

Chuck took Libby's hand and smiled down at her. "Walk to the door with me," he said. "We'll answer it together."

With her head held high, Libby walked with Chuck to the front door. Where was Vera? Did she know Ms. Kremeen and Mother were here?

Chuck pulled open the heavy front door and greeted the women with a wide smile. Libby managed a smile, too, but she knew it wasn't quite as big as Chuck's. How wonderful it was not to tremble and feel faint at the sight of Mother. She had changed to a soft blue skirt and blouse with a single gold chain around her neck. Was she trying to fool Ms. Kremeen and appear to be a nice lady?

"Come in, Ms. Kremeen, Mrs. Dobbs," said Chuck cordially, stepping back with Libby at his side. "Shall we talk in the family room?"

Libby saw the surprise and suspicion on both Ms. Kremeen's and her mother's faces. What were they thinking?

Just as they all sat down, Vera entered with a tray of cold lemonade. "I thought a cold drink on such a hot day would taste good," she said politely as she passed glasses to them.

Libby sat on the floor in front of Chuck's chair. She watched Vera take her glass of lemonade and sit on the piano bench.

"What can we do for you ladies?" asked Chuck.

Ms. Kremeen squirmed uncomfortably. She looked quickly at Marie Dobbs next to her on the couch and then at Libby. Libby smiled and Ms. Kremeen's gray eyes widened.

"I wanted to bring us all together for an amiable meeting," said Ms. Kremeen in a voice that didn't sound quite normal. She cleared her throat. "I know that we can come to terms without a long court hassle, Mr. Johnson. Mrs. Dobbs has changed in the past year while she's been in Australia. She wants her daughter back. You can't, with a clear conscience, deprive a mother of her daughter, can you?"

Libby almost laughed. She was so glad that the words Ms. Kremeen said didn't make her spin into a frenzy of fear as they had before. She could see that Chuck was not upset either.

"Ms. Kremeen, Elizabeth's mother is my wife. She and I are Elizabeth's parents. We prayed Elizabeth into our home. God brought her here. And God is going to keep her here."

"That's the worst piece of garbage I've heard!" cried Marie Dobbs, leaping to her feet. "She is *my* daughter; *I* gave birth to her!"

Ms. Kremeen caught Marie Dobbs's hand and pulled her back down on the sofa. "We are going to stay calm, Mrs. Dobbs."

Marie took a deep breath and locked her fingers together in her lap. "You have four children, Mr. Johnson. You don't need my girl. I have no one."

Just then Kevin rushed into the family room, then stopped, his face flushing red. "Dad, someone's here. And the car looks just like Grandpa's."

"Thanks, Son. You go see if it is. Ask whoever it is to come in and wait in my study. I know Ms. Kremeen doesn't intend to stay much longer."

Libby watched the anger leap into the woman's face as she spoke. "I would prefer to discuss this case without all the religious philosophy you seem determined to use. This is a conversation between adults. We don't need a church discussion. I want you to agree to Marie Dobbs's taking Libby back."

Libby watched the smile on Chuck's face. He crossed his legs and leaned back. "No," he said pleasantly.

"No," said Vera.

Libby wanted to say no too, but she just sat there and watched the puzzled expressions on the two women's faces. They had come for a fight and they weren't getting it.

A commotion in the doorway stopped Ms. Kremeen's next words. Libby gasped as Grandma LaDere walked right into the family room. Albert, her big blue-gray cat, lay in her arms.

"I knew Marie was coming here today," said Grandma LaDere in her sharp voice. "I came to tell you something, Marie. I want you to leave this little girl be."

Libby's eyes widened. Grandma was helping her! She'd driven for more than two hours just to come help her!

Albert squirmed and Grandma set him on the floor. He walked to Libby and rubbed against her, purring loudly.

"Mother, you get out of here and mind your own business," snapped Marie Dobbs, her face brick red. "You don't care about anyone but your stupid cat, so just get out and don't try to help Libby."

Chuck stood up and offered Grandma LaDere his chair. She refused and stood in the middle of the room with her hands on her thin hips. Her black pants hung loose on her skinny legs. A white blouse was half in and half out of the waistband of her slacks. "Marie, you've been nothing but trouble since you were 12 years old. I don't want no more trouble out of you. If you don't get out of here right now, I won't let you in my house again." Mrs. LaDere sniffed loudly. "And where would you go when no man wants you? I could set the police on you for stealing your own sister's money. Would you want me to do that?"

Marie Dobbs leaped to her feet. "Shut up, you ugly old witch! You've hated me all my life. Now you're trying to ruin everything!"

Ms. Kremeen slowly stood and shook her head. "Mr. Johnson, I'm sorry that I started this trouble for you." She took Marie Dobbs's arm. "We are leaving."

Marie jerked free, her eyes blazing. "I won't give up! I am taking my girl and I'm taking her right now!"

Libby stood up and walked right up to her

mother. "Mother, I belong here. You go home with Grandma and try to live happily with her."

Marie lifted her hand to slap Libby, but Grandma LaDere caught it in midair. "No you don't, Marie. Get ahold of yourself and get out before the police come. And I'll call them. Don't you think I won't!" Grandma LaDere looked strong enough to toss Marie out without any help.

Marie grabbed her purse and marched out of the family room. Ms. Kremeen followed her. The door slammed; then all was quiet.

Libby sighed in relief. She turned to her grandma, who suddenly looked like an old, old woman. Libby helped her to the couch, and Albert jumped on her lap. She stroked him and talked to him. Libby wondered if she forgot anyone else was around.

"Thanks, Grandma," said Libby softly.

Mrs. LaDere looked up in surprise. "Don't thank me. I only came because Albert likes you. Don't get no soft notion in your head about me!"

Hurt, Libby turned blindly away and felt Chuck's arms wrap around her.

"Elizabeth has had enough sharp words today, Mrs. LaDere," said Chuck firmly but kindly. "I won't allow more."

Mrs. LaDere stood to her feet with Albert tightly in her arms. "And see that you don't! I'll wait in the car." She strode to the door and slammed it behind her.

Libby didn't know if she should laugh or cry. She leaned against Chuck and smiled weakly as Vera walked to her side.

"It's all over, Elizabeth." Vera smoothed Libby's hair back. "I don't think we'll have any more trouble from your mother."

"Hey, are we going to be kept in the study forever?"

Libby spun around and stared in surprise at Grandma and Grandpa Johnson. She ran to them and hugged them tightly.

After the noisy greeting, they sat down and explained that Mrs. LaDere had called them and told them that she had to get to Libby. "Ordered us to bring her is more like it," said Grandpa, laughing. "That woman can be very determined! But when we learned her reason, we wanted to help all we could."

"Where is she now?" asked Grandma Johnson.

"She said she would wait in the car," said Vera with a chuckle. "I think she used up her 'nice' pill for the day."

"She has a terrible bark," said Grandpa

with a twinkle in his eye. "But I can see the start of a soft spot in her for our Libby."

"She just happens to drop in on the days she gets a letter from you, Libby," said Grandma. "She makes sure we know that she heard from you."

"Why doesn't she ever write to me?" asked Libby, frowning.

"She will, honey," said Chuck, patting Libby's shoulder. "She just needs a little more time and loving from us before she can."

They talked awhile longer, and then Grandpa stood up. He jingled his keys in his pocket. "Elizabeth, we hear you've been taking piano lessons from the famous Rachael Avery. How about showing us what you've learned?"

Libby gladly went to the piano bench and sat down. She smiled over her shoulder. "I still have a lot to learn." And now she had plenty of time to learn it. She opened her book and played the piece she'd been practicing so hard on. She was proud that she was doing her best. Someday Grandma and Grandpa Johnson would listen to her in concert and they'd remember how she'd played for them at home. Maybe Grandma LaDere would want to hear her play too.

Libby smiled. Nothing was impossible with God!

Later, as the Johnsons climbed into their car to drive home, Libby leaned around and peeked into the backseat. Albert sat on Grandma LaDere's lap. He tried to jump off and go to Libby, but Grandma wouldn't let him.

"Good-bye, Grandma. Thank you for helping me." Libby hesitated. She saw the sour look but she continued. "I'll write again soon. I love you."

Grandma LaDere looked up and for just a minute she looked warm; then she frowned. "Shut that door, girl. I don't like the flies you have out here in the country."

Libby stepped back close to Vera. "I love you, Grandma," Libby said again. Even when Grandma turned her face away, Libby felt like shouting. She really did love Grandma LaDere! It was a wonderful miracle from God.

The car stopped at the end of the drive, then pulled out onto the road. Grandpa honked and everyone waved. Rex barked and pressed close to Libby.

"This has been a time of miracles," said Chuck as they walked happily back to the house.

"I love to see God working in our lives," said Vera. She slipped her hand through the crook of Chuck's arm. "I just wonder what's next."

Libby couldn't begin to think of anything else that could happen. So many wonderful things had already happened.

The phone was ringing as they walked into the kitchen. Libby reached for it but Chuck picked it up first. She watched his face as he talked. Who was Dad talking to? Libby sank into a kitchen chair, her heart racing. When Chuck sat down and reached for her hand while he continued listening, she thought she would faint.

Vera walked closer and watched his face.

Finally Chuck hung up the phone. His eyes sparkled. "Call everyone in, Elizabeth. We have wonderful news!"

Libby ran to the door and shouted for everyone to come. What news? Oh, it was hard to wait. Toby seemed to take forever, and Libby wanted to yell at him to get a move on.

When the whole family was gathered, Chuck looked from face to face. Libby could tell he was barely able to contain his excitement. "Children, we have received another

147

wonderful miracle! That was Ms. Kremeen on the phone. She said that Marie Dobbs signed the papers giving us permission to adopt Elizabeth!"

Libby pressed her hand to her pounding heart. Had she heard right?

"Elizabeth," said Chuck, resting his hands on her shoulders and looking down into her suddenly pale face. "Soon you will be Elizabeth Gail Johnson."

"Elizabeth Gail Johnson!" cried Susan and Ben together.

Vera kissed Libby. "Oh, Libby! Elizabeth Gail Johnson! We're going to adopt you. You will really and truly be our very own girl."

Libby blinked hard to keep the tears back. Her dream had finally come true! She would not be Dobb the Slob anymore. She would soon be Elizabeth Gail Johnson!

Tears slipped down her cheeks, but she didn't care as she tried to hug everyone at once. Oh, how wonderful! Elizabeth Gail Johnson! "Thank you, Lord, for making me part of this family!" Elizabeth prayed.

# ABOUT THE AUTHOR

Hilda Stahl was born and raised in the Nebraska sandhills. As a young teen she realized she needed a personal relationship with God, so she accepted Christ into her life. She attended a Bible college, where she met her husband, Norman. They raised their seven children in Michigan, where she lived until her death in 1993.

When Hilda was a young mother with three children, she saw a magazine ad for a correspondence course in writing. She took the test, passed it, and soon fell in love with writing. She wrote whenever she had free time, and she eventually began to sell her work.

The first Elizabeth Gail book, *Mystery at Johnson Farm,* was made into a movie in 1989. It was a real dream come true for Hilda. She wanted her books and their message of God's love and power to reach and help people all over the world. Hilda's writing centered on the truth that, no matter what we may experience or face in life, Christ is always the answer.